END

OF

END OF I.

To Lyndon Park and Paul Maliszewski

MCSWEENEY'S
SAN FRANCISCO

For more information about McSweeney's, see www.mcsweeneys.net

Excerpts of *End of I.* have been published in the following magazines:
*Ann Arbor Review, Bellevue Literary Review, Boulevard, Bridge, Frank, Gulf Coast,
Micro: Fiction for the New Millennium, Noon, One Story, Orchid, Quick,
St. Ann's Review, Story Quarterly,* and *Triquarterly*.

Cover artwork by Daniel Clowes

McSweeney's and colophon are registered trademarks
of McSweeney's, a privately held company with
wildly fluctuating resources.

ISBN: 1-932416-53-6

END OF I.

A NOVEL

STEPHEN DIXON

CONTENTS

FRIEND 1

I. 39

BREAKUP 43

MOTHER-IN-LAW 61

GO 77

PAIN 93

BROTHER 101

DAUGHTER 127

PARTY 139

THREE NOVELS 153

WIFE 175

END 179

FRIEND

TOO LAZY RIGHT now to look at his notes for possible ideas; they're in the memobook he'd have to find first and in the insides of book jackets and covers of books he's been reading or recently read and which are in bookcases and on his night table and other places around the house. And just energetic enough to get out of the easy chair in the living room, where he's been reading a newspaper and occasionally nodding off, to go to his writing table in his bedroom and remove the cover from the typewriter and put some paper in, he tries the following line, which popped into his head whole a minute ago and seemed sufficiently intriguing for him to want to put down to see if it might lead to something he could work on the next week or two or more—for however long it takes, he's saying.

Marty Newman was the name of a friend of his in the third or fourth grade at public school in New York. The line he originally thought of and which brought him here was "Donald Newman (the boy's real name) was a classmate of his in the fourth grade in elementary school, though they always called it 'public school.'" The truth is, they were classmates since kindergarten and had only begun to be friends the last month. Before then, I. never thought of him much, outside of his being the big brain in class. But his best friend for two years, a boy who lived on the block, had gone to Florida with his family that summer—anyway, the kid moved away for good and he was looking for someone to replace him as a friend. Marty came over to his apartment a few times after school. He forgets how that got started. He probably just said to him "Hey, you want to come over to my house after school?" They played in his room and on the street and maybe were becoming good friends when what he's going to eventually get to happened, and he might have gone to Marty's apartment once. No, he definitely went there at least once. Marty's building was on the northeast corner of Amsterdam and 79th. The thing he remembers most about the building, and which caught his attention the first (and maybe only) time he entered it, was that the lobby had the same unusual wallpaper mural, he'll call it (he thinks his mother, an interior designer, called it that too and it was she who said the wallpaper was unusual), that was on the one unbroken wall in their living room (unbroken by windows, fireplace, or entrance): a classical scene in white and different shades of gray of what looked like ancient Roman or Greek ruins: freestanding columns, unfunctioning fountains, caryatids, and atlantes with no entablatures on top, and stone steps, a few with leaves on them, that were cut off and ended in midair.

Marty was an only child, had his own bedroom, a fairly large one with an upright piano in it and a double bed, while he shared a small bedroom with his brother and slept in a bunk bed, which Marty envied him for, I. on top because his brother, being older, got to choose where he wanted to sleep. Actually, I. preferred the top—he liked climbing up a ladder to what he thought of as his own loft—except there was no lamp up there or a table to put his books or a glass or anything else like that on. So when he got in bed he either had to go straight to sleep, play with his miniature cars and planes and tanks and toy soldiers and then when he was through with them pass them down to his brother to put on the night table, or read by the little light cast from his brother's student lamp, his mother called it. He read that much then to say he could have used a lamp just for that? Yes, but not just books; comic books and boys' and *Popular Mechanics* magazines. He once did have a lamp, screwed into the wall above his short headboard. But he kept hitting it with his head when he raised himself out of bed or knocking it out of the wall with his hand when he was having a bad dream, so his mother decided it was safer for him, after the bulb shattered a second time, not to have a bed lamp. Anyway, he played in Marty's room, he forgets with what, but he definitely remembers being sprawled out on a carpeted floor (his own bedroom floor was just wood with a thin rug on it and they had to walk softly at night so not to disturb the tenants below) and playing. An electric train set. Marty brought it out in a box and they assembled it together. He said it had belonged to his much older brother who died of a rare disease about eight years before and whom he didn't remember at all. It was an elaborate set, with tracks that crossed over each other and a tunnel with lights inside and an ice-skating couple who twirled around on a tiny pond and a station with a stationmaster who came out with a lit lantern when the train approached and a train signal and gate that didn't work right. The signal kept going off and the gate coming down right after the train had passed. They made small figures out of modeling clay and put them on the tracks. The aim was for the locomotive, which puffed real smoke, to run over them, but it always ran off the track when its front wheels got stuck in the clay. There were also a couple of plaster cows behind a fence and a roadster with a mustached driver in it which stopped at the train crossing. He forgets what things they did at I.'s apartment. Probably looked at their own hairs under his microscope or played any number of games like jacks and pick-up-sticks or rolled marbles into holes of various sizes he'd cut out of a shoebox, smaller the hole the more points the roller got for getting the marble into it from about ten feet away. His mother no doubt offered them milk and cookies or cake if she was home, or the woman who looked after him if his mother was out working. So he remembers more than he thought. Like the traditional metal railway bridge ("traditional" for electric train sets) the train went over and a figurine of a man sitting off the edge of the bridge with a fishing pole and every thirty seconds or so pulling up and dropping a line with a very small fish hooked to it, though doesn't know what was below, probably just the carpet. But why's he trying to re-create this atmosphere or whatever it is? Who hasn't read a scene like this, two city kids playing with their toys and games in an apartment? What's he trying to say? is what he's asking. He should get to what he said he would about Marty and then go on from there. But the jump to Marty's sudden illness and death would be too great. He wants to set it up, show that a friendship started; suggest, because of that friendship and the way Marty was, I.'s loss. So: cake or cookies and milk at his apartment; he's almost sure of that. He doesn't remember if he got a snack at Marty's. Marty's family had a maid. Not just someone who came in to look after him for a few hours but a woman who worked for them full-time and maybe even lived there. She even wore a black uniform with a half apron (right term?) and a piece of crepe or lace on her head (again, he doesn't know the right name for it), and Marty and she seemed close. There had to be a snack for them and he bets it was something very good. Tea sandwiches on white bread with the crusts removed comes to mind. And the beverage could have been soda (he seems to remember that), something—mainly because his father was a dentist and considered soda and candy the primary causes of tooth decay in kids—he almost never got at home (the only times he had them there were at his birthday parties and when his parents gave their own parties and ginger ale was one of the mixers). Marty's apartment was big and cavernous and very orderly and clean, like the furniture rooms his mother once took him to at the Metropolitan Museum. Even his room was immaculate—he really remembers this, or thinks he does—when they first went into it, which possibly accounts for Marty having to go into his closet to drag out the box with the train set.

He pictures where Marty sat in class. He remembers the day Marty got sick: that was also in class. But first he wants to picture Marty sitting at this desk. He finds it interesting (curious? something else) that he can remember it so vividly: see the classroom, even the apartment buildings across the street from the classroom, and what spot he was seeing all this from. Marty sat in the second row in the next aisle to I.'s left, two rows down, one aisle away from the radiators and windows and plants, one row up from the front of the room and the teacher's desk, if that makes—all of it—any sense, or if any picture, he really means, can be made from it. Certainly the last business about the front of the room and the teacher's desk is redundant. And the plants, he should have made clearer, stood on inside ledges that were below the windows. Marty and he had been in the same class together since—but he said that. But this was the first class they were—that too. So, they were quickly becoming friends, and maybe close ones, when Marty got sick. How close and quickly? Well, not so quickly, and as to "close," he thinks they liked each other a lot. He knows he liked Marty and found him easy as a friend. Easy? Good-natured, easy to be with, other things like that. What others? Just that they got along together, liked doing many of the same things— what else? And he remembers that once they started becoming friends, Marty turning around to him in class and smiling and waving a pencil or just his hand. Indicating he'd been thinking of him, or something like that, right? And sometimes turning around and staring at him deadpan with his chin in his palm and elbow on his desk. And that first and only time when he got sick in class, resting his head on his arms on the desk. The teacher came over. Mrs. Halsey. Stood beside him and said "Martin Newman"— something like this—"are you asleep, feeling ill or simply bored with today's lesson?" He didn't move, eyes stayed shut. A few of the students probably said things like "I think he's sleeping," "I don't think he feels good, Mrs. Halsey," "I bet Marty's faking," and she probably told them to let her handle it please and then announced to the class "I truly do believe (I. remembers how sardonic and even cruel she could sometimes be) that Martin's fast asleep. I hope he's having good dreams." Everyone seemed to laugh. Maybe I. laughed too because he didn't want to be the only holdout or give her the impression he didn't think what she said was funny. She nudged Marty but he still didn't stir. Then her face got serious. That also meant that everyone should stop laughing and look serious. "No, I changed my mind, class. Adults are permitted to do that too, not just children. Martin is too good and attentive a student to fall asleep in class. I'm sure he's ill," and she put her hand on his forehead and said "Martin, Martin, what's wrong?" He opened his eyes and said he was feeling very sick and weak, and looked it. "In that case, so that both we can take care of you and not hold up the lesson any longer, we should"—but get to it already. She chose one of the boys as a monitor and told him to take the wooden pass and escort Martin to the nurse's office. First she said "Who will volunteer to be Martin's escort to the nurse?" Lots of male hands shot up, I.'s among them. Most boys (the girls were mostly afraid of being felt up on the staircases coming back alone or just stopped by boys and talked roughly or dirty to, so the teachers usually didn't pick them if they did raise their hands except to escort other girls) would take any opportunity to get out of class. If they were lucky they'd be asked to wait in the nurse's office with the boy they escorted, though that wasn't why I. volunteered. He did it because he thought of himself as Marty's best friend in class and wanted to help him. He has a picture of Marty—visualization, image, memory, *mental picture*, goddamnit; why'd it take so long to get it?—leaving the room with the boy. He didn't look back at I. or anyone else. Mrs. Halsey, knowing that Marty was too sick to return to class that day, probably asked the boy to take Marty's books with him, and if there was a coat or jacket, then that too, Marty at the time seeming too weak to carry even that.

Marty was the smartest kid in class and had always been the smartest in all the classes I. had had with him. It was Marty, in the third or fourth grade, who first gave him the revelation, he could call it, and he had this right in class, that smart kids are smart from the start—he's talking about *very* smart—and that no matter how hard he worked at his studies he could never come near to doing as well as him and that was probably the way it was going to be for the rest of their student lives. Marty was just naturally very intelligent and he was just naturally only moderately intelligent, and looking back at it now he thinks that thought was the sharpest and deepest he'd had about anything till then. And how did he feel about it at the time? He accepted it, on the spot, and with some pride that he'd come up with it, and also with a bit of relief, he thinks he remembers thinking, because he now knew there wasn't much he could do to change things. Either you had this gift or you didn't, and Marty was proof of someone who had it and I. of someone who didn't. Ever since kindergarten Marty had, it seemed, the correct and quickest answers in class and did the best in tests in every subject. Okay, not since kindergarten—there they mostly played and listened to stories and developed social skills and learned the alphabet by heart and possibly even how to read it and numbers to around thirty and maybe some simple arithmetic—no, that started in first grade; he can actually see himself seated at his school desk with pencil and paper, adding primary numbers (three plus four, etc.)—and how to print your full name. He has no recollection of what Marty was like in kindergarten—how good he was at these things (he suspects very good, even in social skills, since he always seemed self-assured and mature for his age)—but certainly since first grade when they really started doing schoolwork he did exceptionally well. Studies came easy to him, what can he say? He seemed to get a 100 percent or A+ in everything and twice as many stars on the star chart in front of class than anyone else. I.'s average in almost everything, and right through college, was a little less than 75. And as far as stars go, there were months in grade school when he only had two or three green ones—and they were green and not bronze, right?— and no silver or gold. No, there was one subject I. excelled at, so every other month or so he must have got a silver or gold star for: spelling. He was maybe even a little better at it than Marty. He memorized spelling words by writing them down over and over at home and having someone in the family (not his father; he rarely asked him for help with schoolwork; his father didn't have the time or would say when he was reading a newspaper or dental journal or smoking his after-dinner cigar "Your mother and brother's much better at it than me") quiz him the night before a spelling test or bee. When the class was being divided in two for a bee almost all his classmates clamored for him to be on their side. Those were the only times they did that. But he never really learned, no matter how hard he tried to memorize and then use them, grammatical rules and correct punctuation and things like that, and was terrible in reading comprehension. He doesn't think that for the few years it was taught or was part of an exam or end-of-chapter quiz or review that he even knew what reading comprehension was. Teachers would say to him, or maybe one did: "I don't get it. Someone so good in spelling and reading aloud should be so poor in reading comprehension?" and he'd answer, or did once: "I try very hard, thought I had them all right, so I also don't know what happened. But I promise to do much better," not wanting to admit he didn't know what he was supposed to be looking for when reading comprehension was part of a test. Why didn't he ask his brother for help? Probably too embarrassed. Marty also wrote great essays. (But hasn't the point about how smart he was been made? Sure, but just one more; he thinks there'll be something different in it.) Or essays the teachers said were great, for I. found them longwinded and boring and even stuffy and fake. Essays, he thought then, Marty knew few kids his age would understand but his teachers would appreciate. But then he already mentioned the problem he had with comprehension then, so maybe it wasn't Marty's fault entirely, if at all. Teachers loved to read his essays to the class as models for the students to follow when writing or revising their own. Marty also played the piano and violin very well—he once gave a recital at school, going from one instrument to the other—and composed music and sometimes duos for them. His parents were good amateur musicians and were in a string quartet made up only of doctors, and at home Marty and his parents played trios by Beethoven and Mozart and Schubert. These were names I. had recognized by now because of Music Appreciation assemblies in school, the same ten to fifteen short pieces or snatches of pieces played scratchily for two consecutive weeks on the same old record player and which the entire assembly, and this went on right through eighth grade, was then tested on every year, along with the correct spelling of the composers' names. Marty told him—they were talking about what they wanted to be when they were adults—that some people thought he should become a composer and concert pianist or even a violinist, which he said he wasn't as good at, or a college teacher and scholar on any number of subjects, but that his goal, which he'd had since he was five, was to be a doctor. A specialist, though, he now decided, not a general practitioner like his parents, and he gave a long word for the specialty. It had to do with the ear and nose and a couple of other places on the face and it was impossible for I. to get a picture of it as a word, though Marty said it for him and spelled it a few times. "And you?" and I. said maybe become a dentist like his dad, though that was one of the last things he wanted to become and had only said it so he could sort of be on the same professional level as Marty in their conversation. "And maybe the kind that puts braces on kids' teeth. My dad says they make a lot of money." What he really wanted to be, now and later, was a stage actor. He'd been to his first Broadway play that year. It had a boy in it a year or two older than he. He liked the idea of standing out there alone at the end of the play for a few seconds and bowing to all that applause. He couldn't think of anything else a kid could do to get so much appreciation from adults, a few of whom even cheered. He told his parents about it once at dinner—"I'm thinking of taking acting lessons, if you'll let me, and maybe someday be in Broadway plays," and his mother said "That's not the worst thing to aspire to. There have been many great actors and some of the best works in literature have been plays," and his father said "What are you telling the boy? Don't encourage him, even at this age. He'll go into dentistry when he gets older, just like his brother will. He should concentrate, starting now, on doing well in the sciences. Then get into one of the elite public high schools, like his brother has, and eventually both go to NYU dental school, though I'll send them anywhere they want. And after they graduate, join me in my practice and when I retire I'll hand the whole thing over to them without their having to give me a dime." "Being a dentist is a good thing too," I. said, mainly because his father seemed angry at his mother for what she said and he didn't want them to have another argument. "I haven't decided on anything yet for sure; I'm way too young." I. once asked Marty how come he did so well in all his subjects, even Shop. "I'd like to be that way too, or at least do better than I do." "There's no trick to it," Marty said. "I guess I'm just lucky, that I inherited great genes, because both my parents are very smart. But I've always, without really working at it, done well in the serious stuff, and Shop and Art are things I like to do, and Music I've had lots of practice at and love."

Then he got sick, never came back to school. Was in a hospital a while and went home. The class made a get-well card for him out of construction paper—it was the teacher's idea and became part of an art project for a week: everyone made a colored drawing of a get-well card they'd like to receive and then the class voted on the one to go to Marty. It was about ten times the size of a store-bought card and everyone signed it, including several teachers and the principal, and a student who lived on Marty's block dropped it off with his doorman, along with an illustrated book of heroic tales from the teacher and a bouquet of flowers the class chipped in to buy. And Shop couldn't have been something Marty and he talked about being good or bad at; you didn't take Shop till sixth or seventh grade. I. wanted to visit Marty at home, said to his mother "Should I just go to his building and call up from the lobby?" and she said better she call his mother first, and did and was told Marty wasn't seeing any visitors for a long time. Soon after that, Marty's mother sent a letter to the class, which the teacher read. It went something like this (he particularly remembers the tone and also thinking, while listening to the teacher, that he could picture—though he'd never met her—Marty's mother writing it): "To all of Martin's classmates. Martin, as you must know, is convalescing from a very distressful illness. At the moment he cannot respond on his own to your wonderfully thoughtful get-well card and beautiful flowers, which have provided his room with a delightful scent and sight and, as a result, a most welcoming appreciative expression on his face. Dr. Newman and I are quite hopeful that Martin will be well enough in a number of months to return to your class. In the meantime we understand that a few of Martin's classmates have expressed an interest in visiting him. We're afraid his condition doesn't permit that yet and we also want to thank you in advance for your consideration in not attempting to telephone him. Martin does join his parents, though, in thanking you for your lovely sentiments and concern and we wish all of you a joyous and productive school term, and he says hello."

Based on that letter, I. had the feeling Martin would soon die, or live for not that many years as an invalid, always getting worse and worse. He saw him not speaking or smiling or using his hands, and he couldn't imagine him appreciating the flowers and get-well card. He bet he had to be helped to the toilet every time and maybe even have one of those pans stuck under his behind in bed and that he also had to be fed by someone or, as he'd heard very sick people do and saw with his own sister for a short time in the hospital, only through tubes. He told his mother about the letter and some of his worries over it. (Again, what about his father? He would have said something like "Don't worry your head about it, but if you have to, speak to your mother. On things like health and sickness and recuperation, even though I went through some of the same training doctors get in med school, I only know teeth, jaws, and gums, so she's much better to speak to on this.") She said she's sure it's not as bad as he's making it out to be and it's just his imagination that's got the better of him, but to lessen his anxieties she'll call Marty's mother again. "We're adults, so it's okay if I call. As for her letter, she probably wanted to prevent a barrage of calls from classmates Marty didn't know that well but who felt, or their parents did, obligated to ask about his health. Since you were such a good friend of his, I don't think it applied to you." "I was only becoming his good friend," he said, "or maybe only just his friend. Because being a real good friend would take a much longer time. But he's not my only friend. I have others." Sometime later when he asked if she had called Marty's mother, she started to cry. (His mother hardly ever cried in front of him; usually only when she spoke about her dead mother and a couple of times her dead father. And once during a fierce argument with his father, when she yelled at the dinner table—their fights always seemed to be at the dinner table— "That's it, I've had it for good. Stay with you till the children are all grown? You have to be kidding. I'm getting rid of you and taking everything you have, including them, and half of every cent you make in the future," while his father was saying "Calm down, calm down; the kids, and what did I say? I'm always the one who's to blame, but this is nothing we can't hash out alone together," and later she came into I.'s room when the lights were out—his brother hadn't come to bed yet and his little sister was probably asleep—and he was thinking his folks are going to get divorced; this is the worst thing that could happen to him, and said "I got overexcited before when I shouldn't have. Your dad and I have made up, so don't worry, which I know you're doing; you'd have to be.") "You see, it's bad, I knew it," he said. She said "No, just that I thought you have the right to know, but you have to promise you won't speak to anyone about this." "But I can tell; your face; he's going to die," and she said "No no, my darling, the news isn't anything so bad. He *is* very sick, which is why I might look the way I do—it reminds me of when your sister was ill and I hate thinking of anyone so young going through what he is. But both his parents—you know they're doctors?" and he said "Yes, of course, what?" and she said "They think that sick as he is he'll be fine eventually, and the specialist taking care of him—you know what a specialist is?" and he said "Sure I know, what does he say?" and she said "That he'll recover almost completely, though perhaps a little weaker and less mobile—moving around—than before he first came down with what he's got, but it'll take a long time, a year, maybe more," and he said "That's good; I'm very glad. He's a real nice guy, besides being my friend."

He'd lie in bed at night and think of Marty. This was after he died. He always saw the same pictures: Marty turning around at his desk and waving at him with a pencil or his hand. Marty leaving that last day with his escort. (Oh, if he'd only been chosen, he thought. They would have talked on the way to the nurse. He would have remembered a lot of what they'd said. He could have helped him walk to the office—not just carrying his books and coat but holding his arm and sort of guiding him and watching his feet so he wouldn't trip. He might have even put his arm around his shoulders while they sat waiting and said something like "Don't worry, you'll be all right. You're not feeling well now—we all get sick like that sometimes—but you'll be fine in a day or two, I just know. It's probably the grippe; does your stomach hurt too?") The two of them sitting in the middle of Marty's bedroom and playing with his trains, the locomotive toppling over when it hit some tiny claymen and making lots of sparks from the tracks, the woman who worked for them sticking her head in to see if they were playing well and maybe to offer them a snack. Marty resting his head on his arms that last day at school. And one Saturday afternoon, it must have been—that was the only day I. went to the movies then—they went to a movie together and after it had a potato or kasha knish at the little deli next door. The RKO 81st Street theater. RKO Keith, in fact—that's what it was called. He can't remember the main feature they came to see, but thinks it was a comedy. Marty said those were the movies he liked best. The noisy action ones, especially about war and especially when they took place in Asian jungles and the rifles had bayonets on them and the enemy soldiers were Japanese, scared him, he said he was a bit "squeamish" to "confess." I. asked his mother later what the first word meant, and then asked her again when he forgot.

A new transfer student now had Marty's desk. I. asked the teacher if Marty will get it back when he returns. "Oh, do you have information I don't that he's coming back?" and he said "No, I only meant, supposing." She said if he returns before the end of the school year there'll always be another desk for him, and he said "If he doesn't get back his old desk, you think he could sit in the one next to mine? It's empty." "I'd rather not have two buddies sitting so close together. It can turn out to be disruptive. But then again I could make an exception in this case, seeing how neither of you has ever been a discipline problem."

So he looked forward to Marty returning to school, but also felt he never would. He didn't know why but he just had a feeling Marty would stay sick as he is but that if he did get well enough to start studying again, he'd be taught at home or at a special school.

He asked his mother to call Marty's mother again to see how he was. She said she didn't think it a good idea. "My last call, maybe because it came from the mother of her son's friend, seemed to disturb her. I suspect she imagined you playing friskily on the street while her son was cooped up sick at home." "Then his father. I want to know if Marty's gotten better and when I can visit him." She said she'd see what she could do. "But the truth is, all this is a little surprising to me, since you're now acting as if he were the best friend you ever had, while you really didn't know him that long. Anyway, I'm sure he's improving and that you'll be able to see him in a few weeks." "You can't know that unless you call. And if you don't, I'm going to," and she said "Now that I forbid you to do. We're both not sure what it could do to her, even if she is a physician and has more than likely gone through this with some of her patients." "You mean when they got so sick she thought they might die or they died?" and she said "That too, although it doesn't apply to him." "And maybe also because she had another son who died almost before Marty was alive," and she said "Oh my goodness, I didn't know that. That makes everything even worse." He kept after her and finally she called Marty's father at work—she said she didn't want to risk catching his mother at home—and he said Marty's relatively the same: "The good news is he hasn't gotten worse, which means the doctors think they stopped his illness from progressing, and Dr. Newman told me to pass on to you how much he appreciates your concern. It is very nice to see, your concern for Martin." "It's not concern, or maybe I don't know all the meanings for the word. I'm just worried and feel you're all too afraid to tell me the truth." "I'm telling you everything he told me. And I believe him."

He wrote Marty every three weeks or so, telling him about class and what he's been doing when he's not in school: stuff about his brother and sister, books he's reading, nothing about movies he's seen because he didn't want to make him feel he was missing too much by having to stay in bed or wherever he is at home. And the first television set he saw at a neighbor's apartment, though nothing was on it but something called a test pattern, where you just sit and stare at a design, hoping something with live people or cartoons will come on. "Maybe you can get your parents to buy a television set for your home. They're very expensive, my father said, but that would be a good thing to spend time with in the evening when the programs are on, if you don't want to do anything else. And we could watch it together on Friday and Saturday nights when you get all better." Marty's father wrote back once—on his doctor's stationery in penmanship so bad that I.'s mother had to make out most of it for him—saying how considerate he was to write and what an intelligent letter it was. Martin was continuing to improve but hasn't adequately gained back his strength where he can hold a pencil tightly enough to write with, but they expect that to come soon. "He's asked me to thank you for your letters, which he's had read to him several times each and seems to treasure, and that he looks forward to the day when the two of you can play together again.

What a fine lad you are, something I'm sure your parents have told you and which I hope my saying ditto to doesn't embarrass you. When Martin is able to see visitors and no longer must make periodic trips to the hospital, some of them for a week or two, I want you to come by not only to visit him but so that I can finally meet you too. I've always felt comfortable about my son's character, but now I feel even more sure of it, knowing the sort of friend he chooses."

He walked past Marty's building a number of times since he got sick, never just to do it but only when he was on his way to someplace else, like the St. Agnes branch of the public library on Amsterdam or the RKO theater or the Loews 83rd or the Woolworth's on Broadway and 79th, which he liked to walk around in and look at the things it had. He'd stare into the lobby, hoping to see him sitting on one of the two marble benches facing each other there. Or even in a wheelchair, or maybe he'd be in one on the sidewalk or in a regular chair someone had brought outside for him as he'd seen sick people around the neighborhood in, wrapped up in blankets, sometimes only their nose and eyes showing, though those people were always old. Then he'd have the excuse to go in the lobby and speak to him, or speak to him outside if he was in a chair, wouldn't he? He'd have seen him and he could say Marty saw him too and he couldn't just walk by without stopping. That would be discourteous, something his mother told him never to be except to get away from someone acting crazy to him, and maybe even make Marty's sickness worse by it. He also looked up and counted the floors to Marty's apartment—he lived on the tenth or eleventh or twelfth (he knew what number then)—and stared at what he thought was one of his windows. If Marty happened to be looking outside at the time—no, I. wouldn't have been able to see him from so far away—but say he was there, leaning over the ledge a little—it might even have been the ninth or eighth or seventh he lived on, but he doesn't think it was lower than that—he would have yelled out "Marty, Marty, look down, over here, it's me," and waved and shouted till Marty saw him. He once, or maybe more than once, but anyway, when he was walking past the building, wanted to go inside the lobby and with the help of the doorman, or maybe they only had an elevator man there, call up from the switchboard phone and get him on his apartment intercom. To say to this man "I was told by Dr. Newman—Marty's mother—it'd be okay to call from downstairs," and on the phone say, if Marty wasn't the one who answered, he was on the block and wondered, long as he was around here, if he could speak to Marty for a few seconds, he hasn't spoken to him in a long time. Or better than anything, to be invited up—"I'm almost cured," Marty could say on the intercom, "and I was going to call you today to come over"—but knew he could get in trouble at home if his folks found out he'd called from the lobby without permission from Marty's parents.

He thinks it was around three months from the time Marty got sick that their teacher, after all the kids had pledged their allegiance to the flag and sat down, said she had an announcement to make, "the saddest I've ever had to make to a class." She looked sad, but the sad look one gets, he thought, when someone very close dies or a pet, so he knew it had nothing to do with school. He had a feeling, and his stomach started getting queasy and he's sure he got those chills through him, because by now she was choking up a little and fighting back tears, that Marty had died and that's what the announcement would be about. Or maybe the president died. He remembered when Roosevelt died and all the adults were crying everywhere, it seemed, and he just silently watched them, trying to look as sad as them and feeling guilty he couldn't cry. It could have happened this morning and the radio just gave the news. That would be awful if President Truman died so soon after Roosevelt, he thought, but better it be him than Marty, though of course he didn't want anything to happen to either of them. "Class," she said, "you see how difficult it is for me to speak now, so I want your undivided attention. I mean it, because I don't want to have to repeat this if some of you didn't hear. But rather than tell you myself, it might be better if I read the letter that was dropped off for me this morning from the father of your former classmate, Martin Newman, since it's mainly addressed to you." Now the chills must have really gone through him because he remembers thinking something like "Oh my gosh, poor Marty, and we were going to be such good friends." But then thought maybe it's not that and she's only going to read to them that his illness is so bad that he won't be coming back to school this year and maybe not even the next. But that wouldn't make her this sad, would it? It could. Because she might have picked up something from the letter that his condition is so bad that there's almost no chance he'll get better, but that still wouldn't mean there's no hope for him and he won't be able to get even a little better. And from that "little" he can get even a little more better and so on. "You all remember Martin," she said, "or all of you but" and she gave the name of the boy who came into the class after Marty had left and now had his desk. "He was as fine a student as any teacher could wish for and as agreeable as any boy or girl I've had in a class." Now he knew for sure what was coming and he must have felt awful. He might even have cried, or like the teacher, fought back tears. But he doesn't remember crying much at that age except for things like an earache or toothache so bad that nothing for a while could stop the pain. The earache worse than the toothache most times, since with the toothache his father could stop it by taking him down to his office—if it started that night, which it usually did—and treating the cavity there. And when he was very young—up until he was three or four, he thinks— of course he cried a lot, but at things that no longer meant anything to him by the time he was in kindergarten. But at no time, till he became a teenager, he thinks, or maybe even later, did he seem to cry at sad news—and what could that be? Roosevelt, he mentioned. When his mother's favorite brother died—an uncle he liked very much too—and she cried for days and everyone at the funeral was crying, it seemed, but he and a few other kids other than his uncle's children. "But let me read," the teacher said, and held the letter up. "First there's a short passage to me, saying whom the rest of the letter's directed to and what it's about and for me to exercise my judgment if it should be read to the class. I've spoken to the principal and we've agreed it's all right for me to read you this section. 'To Martin Newman's class. I am sorry to inform you that our dear son and your fellow classmate, Martin, died yesterday,'" and he gave the date, which was two days ago. "'Martin's funeral will be held tomorrow,'" which was today. "'I am certain that many of his pals and classmates would like to attend it. We, his parents, earnestly request that because of the enormous tragedy of the events, you respect our wishes to restrict the funeral to Martin's immediate family and our closest relatives and friends. Besides, it takes place during school hours and we wouldn't want you to miss any important work. Thank you, young boys and girls, and also your parents for all your get-well cards and the many thoughtful letters and beautiful drawings Martin received and which we have so far been able to answer only a small token of them. Everything you sent cheered him up considerably while he was so ill. We are both deeply sorry that Martin will no longer be a member of your fine class.'" The teacher then started folding up the letter till it was just a tiny springy square, turned to the window and burst out crying. He looked around the room because it was difficult to continue looking at her. A few of the girls were crying. A boy took an ironed handkerchief out of his shirt pocket and offered it to one of them.

He told his mother about the letter later that day. She said it was the worst thing that could ever happen, a child dying, though a child suffering while dying would even be worse. "I expected it to end like this but never wanted to tell you. Incidentally, there's a very nice obituary of him in the paper, which I only read after you'd gone to school. I'll get it if you want." He asked what an obituary was and then if it had anything about his class and school and she said "It only gives the day he died, how much he'll be missed, and the survivors, which include his four grandparents, and the time of the funeral and that all contributions in his memory can be sent to a certain cancer research foundation and not to send flowers to the home of the bereaved." He thought at the time that "bereaved" meant funeral home and that they didn't want flowers there because it already had enough. "Is there anything I can do for you, dear?" and he said "I'll be okay. It's sad, though, isn't it."

At dinner that night she said "I didn't want to spring everything on you at once, but I went to Martin's funeral today. I had something else planned for the morning but felt the right thing was to be there." His father said "Why? You hardly knew the boy. I don't think I saw him around here once or heard his name before today. What'd he look like?" and I. said "He was here sometimes and I spoke about him a lot. Just, you were always out working, or maybe you forgot. But I know Mommy saw him. He had a big mop of hair and was about my height and a little chubby, but since you never saw him, what I'm saying doesn't mean anything." She said to his father "I did like the boy, and it's true he was quickly becoming a fixture here, and I thought that by going to the funeral I'd not only be paying my respects but standing in for our son. And it was right over here at Riverside Chapel." "The respects you could have done at the kid's shiva, which I'm sure they'll have one," and she said "Those mean much less to me than a funeral. You eat, drink, and kibbitz, and women are usually excluded from the rituals and prayers and only there to serve coffee." "Ah," his father said, "you always had a morbid nature. Why else would you read the obit page first thing every day," and she said "You do too," and he said "I've got ten years on you so I'm looking for people my age I grew up with and knew." I. said to his mother "You never said how the funeral was," and she said "I didn't? Very sad, as you can imagine. Everyone weeping, I think even the rabbi and the men who work there," and he said "Any children at it?" and she said "None I saw." "Was he in a coffin?" and she said "Of course, what else? It was open till the ceremony began." "Let's talk about something else at supper?" his father said and I.'s brother said "I agree. It's not appropriate dinner conversation." Later, while I.'s mother was washing dishes and he was drying them—his night to—he said "About Marty today, did he look okay in the coffin? Not sick or scarred up or scary?" and she said "He looked handsome, not sick at all, just as he did the last time I saw him, but of course more peaceful. But he was always sort of a placid boy, wasn't he? And he thought "Placid, placid," no, doesn't know the word, but said "Right. But when I saw him in class that last day he looked sick. Like he had a stomach- and headache, though not an earache, because then you look in terrific pain, your face. What was he wearing?" and she said "You really want me to go in to that?" and he said "I'm interested. I wouldn't ask if I could have been there," and she said "A white shirt and tie and suit." "I didn't know he owned a suit. What boy does?" and she said "At least I'm assuming it was a suit. Because the bottom lid of the coffin was closed I couldn't' see any part of Martin from a little above the waist down. But his jacket looked like the kind that had matching pants. It had three buttons, and all of them buttoned, and just seemed to be cut like a man's suit jacket, though in this case a little man's." "You saw him so close to see the buttons?" and she said "Like most everyone there I went up, before the services began, to walk past the coffin." "Maybe it was just another kind of sports jacket for a boy and he had nothing on below," and she said "He'd have to have something on. I'm sure it was pants and probably even more: undershorts and socks. They wouldn't let him be half undressed." "Do you say anything or touch him when you walk past?" "You could say something, but mostly you just look. Though some people—probably close relatives—put their hands in, so I suppose they touched him. And what seemed like the woman who worked for his family, leaned over to kiss him." "I knew her. She was strict with Marty but nice to me. If I was there I wouldn't have touched him. I'd be afraid I'd mess up something and also how his skin would feel. Was his hair combed?" and she said "Why do you ask?" "Because he never liked to and I want to see how it turned out. He had tough hair to comb, like wire and very long for a boy, so I bet it got tangled and hurt him when he was forced to comb it." "What I recall is that it was flat and parted." "Then it wouldn't have looked like his. His hair was always all over the place and a lot of it on top standing up. He also hated taking haircuts. Maybe they gave him one to get his hair down. But he told me that. He was afraid barbers would nick his ears and neck, which once happened, and he bled." "No, his hair was combed, didn't seem freshly cut, and where he had a little pompadour, and he looked quite handsome." "You said that before, but he couldn't have. He was pudgy, almost fat, and his hair was hard as wire and his face was never handsome. I suppose they did something to him there too. The people at the funeral home who took care of him before they stuck him in the coffin. Maybe even dressed him in some man's old suit; a dead man's." "I'm sure they don't do that. If he didn't already have a suit, then his parents probably bought him one for the funeral." "What a waste of money that'd be. That's why I think it was a sports jacket he was in. I once saw in his closet and he had a few of them, and one was camel's hair, same color and everything like Dad's overcoat." "His jacket today wasn't camel hair," and he said "I know that. I'm only saying if I had been there I might have recognized the jacket as one of those I saw." "But you know why they didn't want children there," and he said "Still, it would only have been a few of us. They could have put us way in the back, but I don't want to talk about it anymore." "I understand. I know how you feel now, so if you want I can finish drying for you and you can do something else with your time," and he said "No, it's my job. I just don't want to talk while I'm doing it." Of course the conversation only went something like that.

He passed Marty's building lots of times after that when he was still a boy and thought of him each time. Once: You're coming up to Marty's old building. This time don't think about him, but you already did. Another time he wondered what Marty's parents had done with his room. Maybe turned it into a guest room or study for one of them or a television room as people had started doing then. Or kept it the way it was when Marty was alive minus the hospital bed if they'd had to put one of those in. Minus all the medical stuff that must have been in the room when he was sick. Things for breathing, these bottles on poles for feeding, a wheelchair, and maybe some other medical equipment and a sit-down potty. In other words, where it looked like a hospital room. But after all these things were taken away and the old stuff moved back, kept it the way I. remembered. He'd heard of people doing that, especially parents for their kids. Would his parents have done it to his sister's room if she had died, which they said for a while she came very close to doing? He didn't think so. Their apartment wasn't as big as Marty's, they also had three kids compared to Marty's parents' one, and he—or if his brother had wanted it, then his brother—would have got her room. How would he have felt sleeping in a dead person's room? Not good at first, he thought, but he would have got used to it, since he'd be glad to have his own room and a single bed, if his brother didn't have it moved into his. It must be very hard, he thought then, for Marty's parents to walk by his room, and worse if it had been put back the way it was. To picture him on his bed reading, for instance, or at his desk studying or typing—he had a real typewriter, something I. wanted once he fooled around with Marty's, but his mother said he should wait till high school; playing on the floor, and so on. Having a snack there, which I.'s mother, who said she was sorry but she was "phobic" about rodents and roaches, never let any of their kids do except when they were sick and had to stay in bed most of the day, and then they had to be extra careful with their drinks and crumbs. Marty had a music stand, so standing before it and practicing the violin, and of course sitting at his piano and playing. Did they clean his room when they cleaned the rest of the apartment, he thought, or had the woman do it, the one who kissed Marty in his coffin? Did they even keep the woman after Marty died, he thinks now. There might not have been enough work for her, so she had to be let go or just came in once a week, he'll say, to clean. Spring-cleaning was big in I.'s apartment, he thought then, his mother and a woman she hires just for that, spending a couple of days at it. Fall-cleaning too, he thinks now, when all the windows were washed inside and out and mirrors polished and drapes rehung and slipcovers taken off the living room couch and chairs and the bedspreads changed from light to heavy again and floors waxed and everything in the kitchen cabinets removed and the food bottles and jars wiped and protective oilcloth in the cabinets washed down with an ammonia solution till there was nothing sticky or greasy on it. So did they spring-clean Marty's room, he thought then, when they did the rest of the apartment, which he's almost sure they did because the place was always so clean? That is, if they did put his room back to the way it was before Marty got sick. Of course they'd spring-clean it and just normally clean it when the rest of the apartment was cleaned, if it had been turned into a study or guest room. Did either of Marty's parents, he thinks now, if they had put his room back to the way it was, ever lie on his bed and think of him; think of both their dead sons, since the older one once had the room to himself too, or just let thoughts of anything come, hoping they'd be about their sons. Did they play Marty's radio or record player while they were in the room, he thought then, some of his 78 rpm records, he thinks now, which were mostly albums of Broadway musicals and classical piano pieces? Did they sometimes tinkle on his piano, he thought then—either of them, he thinks now, since both were serious amateur string musicians and the ones I. has known also know how to play the piano fairly well? Did they take out of the piano bench Marty's music sheets and books and play from those, or something he might have composed? Did they sit at his desk, he thought then, and just stare at his typewriter, or get from somewhere, he thinks now—probably from one of his desk drawers—something Marty had written on his typewriter and read it in that room? That might have been too sad a thing to do—it would for him now if he were in the same situation—and if they did start to read something of his, he doubts they got very far before they had to put it down. Did they close Marty's blinds from time to time, he thought then—or were they shades, he thinks now, and not just to keep the sun out, as I.'s mother used to do in the summer so the room would stay cool? If they did turn the room into something else, he thought, then Marty probably pops into their heads less now when they walk past it or are in it than if they'd kept the room the way it was.

He was on Broadway in the Seventies—this was around four years after Marty died—heading back to the bakery he delivered orders for, when he thought he saw Marty walking about twenty feet in front of him. The boy was holding a thick book and was with a man who was carrying a Sunday *Times* and looked kind of distinguished with a bushy mustache and in a fedora and tweed overcoat and silky scarf, which was what he thought Marty's father would look like based on the note he wrote to their class and being a doctor who played the violin and lived on such a fancy block. So it was Sunday (I. only worked weekends and holidays then) and he thought when he caught a profile of the boy My God, there's Marty, and wanted to shout out his name and catch up with them. This lasted—from the time he first thought it could be Marty till he realized his mistake—about ten seconds. Then he slowed down but continued to walk back to work behind the boy who looked like Marty had a few years before, which of course, he thought, he couldn't look like now if he were alive. His face would have changed a lot, just as his own had, and he'd be taller—much taller (unless his sickness had somehow stopped it, he thought) because of his first big growth spurt, which I. and all his friends had gone through except one little guy who didn't have his till he was sixteen and even that wasn't much of one: the boy stayed quite short. And he wouldn't be wearing those younger boy's clothes, and so on. The thick book, though; that'd be him. This has happened a couple of other times to I., but when he was an adult. One he can't remember. All he knows is that it was also on the street and it took a good half minute to realize his mistake and that for a few seconds he was about to run up to this person and kiss her. So he does remember. A cousin who'd died several years before he thought he saw her. He had gone to her funeral, in fact, but only because his mother asked him to take her. Otherwise, he would have stayed away. He can't stand going to funeral homes and cemeteries and synagogues. No problem in understanding why. Most synagogues he finds ugly, dreary, and gawdy-looking, though maybe his not wanting to be in them has something to do with his having had to study for his bar mitzvah in an Orthodox one almost every day after school for two years and the strictness and sometimes meanness of the rabbis and tutors there. One used to hit his open hand with a pointer; another liked to grab him by his ear or around the back of his neck and march him into the classroom. They thought they were being funny and these were maybe the only times he saw them laugh. His father said he'd speak to them about it but he doubts he ever did. Cemeteries and funeral homes are other dreary places, of course, but it could also be the thoughts he always gets in them that he'll, or when they were alive, his parents will, or his children or wife or brother end up like the person being buried and with all the sickness, pain, and wasting away that comes before it, and so forth. Hospitals he also doesn't like going into, but when he has to—when he has to for all of them, but more easily hospitals—he does. No, that's not true of hospitals. Think of his sister and father and recently his mother and sister-in-law, and in between them a couple of close friends. When he visits he usually steels himself in the elevator for what he's about to see except if he's going to the maternity floor, and that he hasn't done in years. Churches he has no trouble going into, but goes solely for the architecture and art and lots of times to sit in them, when nothing was going on in the church, to get out of the city heat or just to think. And the second time in a movie theater lobby. A man rushing out of the inside doors after the movie ended—I. and his wife were waiting for the show to break and theater to empty out so they could go in—and he clutched her wrist and pointed at the man and probably looked startled and she said

"What?" and he said "Wait, what am I, nuts? We went to his memorial years ago. But for a second I could have sworn it was—" and she said "The man who just flew past? You thought it was Boris? But the height, cheekbones, and build… Boris was getting big as a balloon and this fellow was a rail. I don't see those two looking that much alike except for the slicked-back sort of greasy hair and I think the drinking man's nose, and I never saw Boris move half that fast," and he said "If you didn't think they looked alike, how come you knew I was referring to Boris?" and she said "Because his was the only memorial I ever went to with you."

About ten years ago he said to his mother "Do you remember a boy I used to know as a kid, Marty Newman, or as the adults always called him, Martin?" and she said "Not right off." "I didn't think you would; it was so far back. You were what at the time, around forty, so more than ten years younger than I am now. That always gets me, that matching-up-the-ages thing, or whatever you want to call it, yours or Dad's with mine when you were my present age or, in this case, when I'd compare myself to you or Dad when I was also forty. Anyway, I saw an obit in the *Times* the other day—" and she said "Why are you reading those for? You're still too young to bother, and they can be depressing no matter what age you are. I doubt I started reading them, except to get the time and place of funerals I had to go to, till I was sixty," and he said "Come on, you and Dad read them almost religiously long before. I even remember arguments you had over them, or one, where one of you accused the other of something, but I forget what. Reading them first thing in the paper, maybe. And I don't know; some of the obits of important historical figures are interesting. Also of lesser-knowns who made a small impact on things. Writers, of course, but especially baseball players and movie actors and actresses of my youth and heroes in World War II. I like to read of their exploits in battle and famous escapes from prison camps and then what they did after the war. Usually they worked in a printing plant for forty years or were career officers who retired at fifty or so and went back to school. With the historical figures I can catch up on contemporary history, and the ballplayers bring me back to when I loved the game. As for the actors, I guess the same as for the ballplayers, but for movies. I never read the paid obits; just the bylined ones written by the paper's writers. This one was of an inventor of a plastic shield that revolutionized the space industry, it said. Made it possible to advance it by about ten years to get us to the moon before the Russians. Not that any of that interests me, though if what the obit said he did is true it's definitely history. Or that I would have read it if the man didn't have the same name, maybe even right down to his middle initial 'p,' as my friend from public school." "Reacquaint me. What you said got me a little lost. Which friend was this? You had so many." "No I didn't. I never did and still don't, but I had more then than today. I'm not someone who ever befriended people easily, though as an adult it's also been people having trouble befriending me. I'm talking of the boy—full face, somewhat stocky body, huge shock of unruly hair? Brilliant; musically gifted; always first in his class scholastically, and whose funeral you went to. We only started being friendly in the fourth grade when for a month or more he came over to our apartment fairly regularly and same with me to his, but much less. Then he got sick and our budding friendship got cut off, and we never saw or spoke to each other after he was taken home from school one day. His parents wouldn't let me speak to him on the phone or visit him—no kids. I suppose for good reason, or I hope so, for I felt I could build up his spirits if I saw him and because of that his recuperative powers. He was too sick to be seen, they said. Though if that was so, how come he was allowed to stay at home for months before he died?" "Who knows," she said. "Maybe because they had nurses and equipment and such there. But excuse me, what funeral? When did I ever do that? Why would I go to one of a boy you said was only becoming something like a good friend to you?" "I've wondered that myself. You said you were representing me at it. That seemed okay as a reason then. Now I think maybe you were despondent about some other things at the time. Something in your own family related to sickness and possible death—your younger brother? I don't know—and you went because the funeral of a young boy would be sadder than just about anything. And because of my connection to him and that you'd also known him, you felt you had a legitimate reason for being there." "I don't get it. That I might be so sad about something that I'd want to be even sadder?" and he said "Maybe we should forget it. I thought I was on to something, but it never quite emerged because I didn't think it out enough or express it well and now I've totally lost it. What I do remember is coming home from school after our class was told the news that Marty had died—and remember it clearly, though you know as well as I that even that kind of memory can't be trusted sometimes. And you told me—or this could have been later, at night. I think so. That you'd read his obituary in the *Times* that morning and went to his funeral and I asked you lots of questions about it—and you told me. But all right, I could be mistaken. It was at Riverside Chapel, though. Does that help?" "Almost all the funerals I go to are at Riverside, but I've never in my life been to one of so young a child. And when you talk of what great prospects he had because of his intellect, it would've been even more heartbreaking a funeral, so one I'd remember." "He *was* that smart; in everything. I'm sure he would have been an eminent scientist, doctor, college professor, or dean. Certainly now at the top of his profession, and maybe even a fine musician and composer of serious music. He was the one who proved to me—a theory I think I had since the first grade—that people who are effortlessly brainy—not creative or artistic so much, though he was that too, but just brainy—are probably that way from birth, or close to it. No, from birth. It's just in them and then when they begin talking and thinking about things and conveying their ideas and what they've figured or are figuring out, it immediately becomes obvious." "You're also very smart," and he said "I'm not so smart and whatever smarts I do have I had to work hard for. But he, in addition to everything else, was a great kid: cheerful and funny and modest and without a mean or competitive or ungenerous feeling in him. I just wish we had become friends long before. He was in public school with me right from the beginning and I think in every one of my classes, so I had the opportunity. But I was probably busy with other kids or jealous or intimidated by his brains or saw him as a geek and avoided him because my friends did, so never could get around to appreciate him. I don't know what changed it. Maybe for a while I was on the outs with my other friends. But you still don't remember him from anything I said?" and she said "His name and the incident you speak of and that he came to our house a few times, no. But I am getting old, you know. It's possible you would've had better luck if you had asked me this ten to twenty years ago." "It wouldn't have come up. This other Martin Newman, the inventor, was still in the pink of life then, I presume." "Who's that?" and he said "The man who died a few days ago and whose obituary I read and which got me started thinking of my boyhood friend Marty." "You sure this man isn't your old friend Martin Newman?" "How could he be? You told me what he looked like in his coffin, though you don't remember that now. There was an obituary of him more than forty years ago. He got sick and I never saw him again in or out of class and he died. You in fact used to speak to his mother on the phone about his sickness, and then, because I think she got too distraught to talk about it, his dad. Both of his parents were doctors? They lived on West 79th? You don't remember any of that either?" "No, not really, not that I don't believe you. Funny how the mind works, right?"

I.

HE SAID "HI, how are you, I've seen you so many times on the block, at Fairway, I'm always running into you, so I thought I'd say hello," and stuck out his hand and gave his name: Lewis. Guy seemed nice, nice smile, not a crunchy or flabby handshake, nice appearance, intelligent face, maybe—who knows: somebody on the block, finally, he could talk to about something else but the block, weather, sports, movies, what's in the newspaper. In other words... well, other things. They talked. Liked the guy immediately. He didn't hog the conversation, push his views. When he found out what I. did, not for a living but for his enjoyment or whatever you want to call it, he spoke about the books he's reading, good ones, and poetry and a collection of essays. That he sometimes dabbled in writing himself but knows he's no good, and alas, he said, he's just a lawyer, and I. said "So what's so wrong with that? Abe Lincoln was a lawyer; there had to be some other good people who were lawyers," and they laughed, and I. thought Stupid joke; nice of him not to take me up on it. Then Lewis said he had to go and hoped to bump into him again, and maybe one afternoon, or weekend, really, since he's always busy with work day and night during the week, they could meet for coffee and chat some more, and I. said "I'd like that; I enjoyed our talk." So he walked away from him, thinking A real nice guy, affable, smart; maybe he was right before: a possible friend. Because almost more than anything, what he likes is a deep stimulating conversation with someone who likes to listen as much as he likes to talk.

He saw Lewis a week later leaving a brownstone about ten doors down from his. He seemed angry, or maybe that was just what it looked like the hundred feet away from him he was. But wait a minute. Shorts on such a cool day? And no shirt? What's the guy, crazy? Suddenly Lewis darted into the street and shouted at a car that passed. The car stopped. "You goddamn bastard," Lewis said, running up to it. "You're the one keeping me from sleeping and working with your goddamn noisy car. Honking, beeping, revving it up, playing your dumb lousy radio music loudly." The driver rolled down his window and said "What? Come again? What're you talking about?" A car stopped behind this car, honked. "You too," Lewis shouted, and went over to the driver's side. "Put some clothes on, you idiot," the driver said. "Idiot? I'll show you, freaking head," and banged the hood with his fists. The car started backing up. The car in front drove off. "All of you with your noise, clamor, shouting, music, tumult, commotion, brouhaha, brou-*ha-ha*," shaking his fists in the air, then grabbing his hair on the sides and pulling it and getting on his knees and shouting with his eyes closed and facing the pavement "I can't stand it, I can't stand it." I. didn't know what to do, started to pass, then thought No, go, help the guy, and went over to him—people were looking out the windows of buildings and from the sidewalk, cars had stopped because he was in the middle of the street and they couldn't pass, some honking—and said "Lewis, get up, go to the sidewalk, into your building, cars are trying to get through, and it's too cold out, the way you're dressed, and what's wrong; really, what's wrong?" and put his hand on his shoulder and Lewis snapped his shoulder away, looked fiercely at him and said "Who do you think you are, you arrogant bastard, telling me what to do?" "You need help, buddy; really, let me help you," and Lewis said "You must mean someone else," and shook his fist at him and went into his building.

BREAKUP

THEY RARELY DISCUSSED; they just agreed and did. One or the other of them: "Dinner tonight?"—"You bet." "Like to go to a movie?"—"Sure, name the time." "Drop by, I'll be in all day"—"I'm on my way." "I'd like to stay home alone tonight if you don't mind"—"Me? Has it ever been a problem? I'll talk to you tomorrow." "I know it's late but I'm feeling lonely for you. Can I come over?"—"Of course." Then: "I'm afraid I'm tied up tonight, so maybe another time." "What? How come?" "I'm busy, that's what I'm saying." "I know, but since when, and doing what?" "Something." "You mean 'someone.' A man?" "Okay; yes." "I expect it isn't business." "No, it isn't." "But where and how did this all take place?" "It just has; I'm sorry. But call me, all right?" "For what?" "Who knows what can happen, or won't. We'll see." So he called: "I'm afraid," she said, "it's more serious than I thought." "You mean with this other man?" "You know that's what I was saying." "I didn't; I don't. First we were seeing each other almost every day or night. Then you hit me with this in a matter of days." "Like I said, or intimated: it just happened; somebody I met. I can't quite explain it; boom, and everything changed. I didn't want to hurt you, obviously I have, and you can't know how terrible I feel about that." "So we're not going to see each other again?" "In the way we did, I don't see how." "Screw you, then," and he hung up.

He showed up at her door that night. "How'd you get in the building?" "Is anybody with you?" "I asked you a question." "Rang a whole bunch of bells." "That's unfair to my neighbors." "Don't worry, the bells were all for the top floors. And right now you think I care about your neighbors?" She wouldn't let him in. "Then come out to the hallway so we don't have to talk through the door." "I don't want you to make a scene." "I won't." He did. She went back into her apartment, locked the door. He put his ear to the door, didn't hear any talking, said "So you're alone. Just let me in or come out to the hallway again or meet me for coffee someplace and I absolutely promise this time not to raise my voice or do or say anything even remotely unreasonable." She didn't answer. He knocked, rang the bell, said her name several times, went home and called and called and she finally picked up the phone and said "Please stop calling me. We said everything we needed to in the hallway and any further discussion of the matter isn't going to change things." "You don't have to tell me that. I know I'm only making it worse. But the truth is, it can't be worse. I feel miserable. Worse than miserable, whatever the word for it is. I want to see you. I want it to be like it was. I want it to be even more than that. I want to live with you, marry you, have a baby with you." "You said all that in the hallway and I'll say again what I said then: 'Don't be absurd.' It's even more unquestionably the wrong time to propose such things." "And if I'd have said it before—not in the hallway or this call but before you met this new guy?" "It would have been way premature." "Go way-premature yourself, you bastard." "Oh? And now you're going to hang up?" He hung up.

He went to her building the next night. Went through hell thinking about her the whole day and last night. She wasn't home. Or she was but didn't answer when he rang from downstairs. He went outside and looked up at her windows. Lights were on but she often left them on when she left the apartment for an hour or two. He could have rang some of the other tenants' bells to get into the building but that would have been just like the previous night, and if she was in he was sure she wouldn't answer him through her door. He thought of yelling her name from the street, but that would just get her mad. He sat on the front steps, waiting for her to come home or leave the building. About an hour later he saw her coming down the street with a man. He stood up, didn't know what he'd say to her. Maybe just "Hello. Can we talk a minute alone, please?" After that, if she consented, what? She must have seen him in the few seconds he shut his eyes to think what to say to her, because she and the man were gone. He ran to the corner, only place he thought they had time to disappear around, though didn't know what he'd say to her when he got to it if she was still there. Maybe just "Wait up; can't we talk for a minute, or even less? Whatever you want. I promise I'll be sane, reasonable, and calm." She and the man were nowhere around.

He called her when he got home. Thought of stopping

at a bar along the way for a drink or two, but then thought Go straight home; you have plenty of booze there if that's what you think you need before you call her or you just want to get drunk. Her phone rang and rang. That night and the other nights and during the day. Then she had an answering machine taking her calls, with a very simple message: "I can't come to the phone right now. Leave a brief message or just your name and phone number and I'll call back as soon as I can." She was the first person he knew who got an answering machine for home. A month or so ago she said "They're so impersonal, I'll never get one. Someone can't reach me, he'll call back. If he doesn't, then it can't be too important. But I have to spend half an hour, if I happened to have been out a while, listening to callers jabber away as they do on my machine at work, most of them repetitively and incoherently till I'm forced to cut their messages off?" He said on the machine "It's me and I'd like to speak to you. Thanks, goodbye." "Please don't say it's useless. Call, please?" he said the second time. The third time: "Please reconsider going with this guy and coming back to me." The next time: "I know I'm making a fool of myself with these calls." The next time: "The heck with succinctness; I meant to say 'an idiotic ass, creep, and pitiful fool of myself.' Right? I'm not wrong about that, right? Goodbye." The next time: "Okay, okay, this is the last time I'll call. You're not in, you'll never be in, in reality, metaphorically, and anything else. Besides, you're probably even screening your calls when you are in, if your machine's able to do that, to see if it's me. Well, it is, in all my ignominious glory and self-lacerating and -defeating fatuousness ineptitude. Sorry; too long and incoherent and repetitious a phone message. Goodbye." The next time: "It's only me; who'd you expect?" The next time: "Just me again." The next: "Me again." All this in one night. Didn't say anything the last call; just quietly put the receiver down right after he heard the beep to speak.

He looked up at her window a few nights after that. He'd tried forgetting her since he'd stopped calling her, but couldn't. Living room light was on, but again: didn't mean she was home, though she could be. Maybe her habit of leaving the lights on when she was out had changed since she met the new guy. But why? He didn't know. The man might have told her it was a waste of money and unecological and other things and his argument was a lot better than the one I. had given her on the same subject a while ago or she simply wanted to please him early in their relationship by going along with what he said. Oh, could be anything. He rang her bell from downstairs. If she answered he was going to say "It's me, can I come up for a minute?" A man said on the intercom "Yes?" "Nothing. Wrong apartment. Sorry." "I bet," the man said. Was it possible he had rung the wrong bell? He didn't think so but he could have. He seemed to remember pressing the bell where her name was but his finger could have got the one above or below; it had done it once before. He rang her bell again, or for the first time. "What," the man said, "you again?" "No. Sorry. I now see it's the wrong building I'm in. I thought this was number six." "Sure," and the man hung up. And who did he think he was fooling? If she was home, and she probably was, chances are she would have been near the intercom—

at least that second time—and heard his voice. Getting caught up in all this, he forgets such things. So he now looked even more hopeless to her, but so what, and maybe his pitifulness will somehow make her sympathetic and responsive to him. But that's ridiculous, though one never knows for sure what can move someone to change her mind.

He went home and wrote her a long letter and dropped it in the mailbox in front of his post office that night. It spoke about his love and longing for her and the wonderful memories he has of their being together and gave several examples: on the Central Park merry-go-round, their side-by-side horses, which they took their time choosing to find the most striking pair, moving up and down at the same time, "no sly allusion meant by that image either, I swear"; day they spent on Fire Island and the three-hour solitary walk on the beach looking for old druggist bottles in the dunes: "We only found one, though with a stopper—we each wanted the other to have it and chose and I won—but I don't know when we ever felt closer or had more fun, or so it seemed to me"; weekend at a lodge in the Catskills that, he's sorry to say, she had to pay for most of since he was practically broke at the time, "but you felt you needed a break in the country and I wanted to be at a place like that with you, with a working fireplace in the room and wood walls in the library and halls, so we went"; night they got snowed in at her apartment and the power outage in that part of the city for twelve hours "and we had to get around by candlelight and, when the last candle went, just feeling around with our hands." He wrote several more letters the next few days, all of them long. Even though he didn't expect her to answer any of them, he went down to his building's vestibule every day a little after the time the mail usually came, hoping there'd be a letter from her. His last letter ended: "I'm sorry but I had to get all of this out of my system and you, unfortunately, had to take the brunt of it, if that's the right use of that term. Though by now—if you ever did (if you even opened my letters other than for the one I typed your address and put no return name and address on a different-sized envelope than I normally use)— you're no doubt not even reading them. This will be my last, though, I promise, or sincerely hope. I wanted to say then 'Stop me before I write another one,' but I'm sure I've used that line another time and even if I haven't, you can't be in any mood for a joke, or sad attempt at one, from me."

He bought a book the next week she once said she wanted to read and own but it was too costly and she'd wait till it came out in paperback or get it from the library. He told himself not to, that it was stupid, futile, absolutely wrongheaded and so on, but he got it weighed and stamped at the post office and sent it to her. He was a little surprised she didn't mail it back or just return the package unopened with her name crossed out and an arrow pointed from it to his in the top left corner and something written on it like "addressee unknown, return to sender." But she might have thought that either of those could have been seen as some kind of communication from her, which would encourage a response from him, or certainly more of a chance for one than doing nothing would.

A few months later he dropped off a manuscript at a small publisher in her neighborhood. He'd been thinking less and less of her the last few weeks but still hadn't gotten over her. He could have mailed the manuscript but thought What the hell, bring it down personally, save a day or two getting it there and know that it arrived safely, and who knows, maybe he'd bump into her. After he delivered the manuscript he thought maybe she was in her local supermarket, and went to it a few blocks away. If he met her on the street along the way he'd say "Hi, what a nice surprise; I just dropped something off at a publisher's on Hudson and was going to your supermarket to buy a couple of things." If he saw her in the market he'd say "Hi, what a nice surprise. I just dropped off a manuscript on Hudson and thought I'd come in here before I headed home. I remembered it was a much better market than the one around me, especially for cheese." He picked up a shopping basket, looked through the entire market for her, and put the basket back. If he saw her when he was leaving he'd say "Hi, I was in the neighborhood, remembered they had some good cheese in here, but they didn't have the one I wanted." The Italian bakery, he thought, maybe she was there. It was a block from her building and she seemed to go to it for something almost every day. If she was there he'd say "I was in the area, delivering a new manuscript to a publisher down here, when I remembered what great hard cookies this place made—you know, the long thin ones with almonds in them; I forget their name." He saw through the store's front window she wasn't inside. He went to her block, though it was in the opposite direction from the subway he'd take home, hoping to see her on it or in her window from the street. If he saw her there he'd turn front and keep walking, hoping she'd see him and call out to him. If she was on the street he'd say "My God, what a surprise… Well, I don't know why I should think it should be one, since this is your block. But I was on my way to Victorio's—you know, for these long hard cookies they make so well and you intro-duced me to—biscotti, that's it, and especially for the ones with almonds—after dropping off something at Big Dip Press on Hudson." She might know of the publisher or ask what number Hudson and then see he could have gotten to the bakery by a much shorter route. He'd think of some-thing, though, to explain why he was on her street, when he saw her leaving her building. She didn't see him, or give any sign she did—he was across the street—and he thought just let her go, but yelled out her name. She turned to him. "Oh, hello," she seemed to say, and seemed to be smiling, and raised her free hand a little as if she was going to wave it, but lowered it again and just stood there. She was waiting for him to cross the street, he thought, so he did. "What do you know," he said. "I mean, that's such a senseless expres-sion, but when I saw you I really did think what a surprise. Of course I was aware you lived on this block, but it never entered my mind you'd be around. The chances of it… Anyway, I was on my way to… coming from, I mean… well, coming from and on my way to… ah, what does it matter why I'm here. How are you doing?" "Fine," she said, "and you?" "Fine, good, couldn't be better, really, and such a beautiful day. Great for walking; anything." "It is nice out." He asked about her job; she asked about his work. He asked about her father and she his mother. "Have you trav-eled recently," he said, "or anything like that?" and she said

"What, in the few months since we last spoke? If you mean through work—" and he said "No, I meant personally, but also work, but I don't see why it should be any of my business. Me, nothing; the city, always the city, and who's got the time and money for it; traveling, I mean." He wanted to say talking to someone he bumps into on the street always does this to his conversation, makes it rushed and innocuous and him somewhat inarticulate. Instead, if she's got the time, would she like to sit down for a coffee someplace? But wanted some indication she'd be receptive to the idea. So far, since what he thought might have been a smile from her when he yelled out her name, she looked serious, even somewhat suspicious, as if his being on her street and catching her leaving her building was no accident. "So," he said, "I don't mean to take up your time. I'm sure you're on your way somewhere, I am too, so I'll see you." "Would you consider delaying wherever you're going so we can sit down someplace for coffee?" "Sure, that'd be nice. But you'll want tea, won't you? Your habits on that haven't changed." "No, but I said coffee because it's shorter than saying both. I know, just 'tea' would even have been shorter—you see, I know by now what you're going to say or at least how your mind works—but then you would have said you'll have coffee." "I might have. You can't be too sure you got a lock on what I'll say or think, even if this time you were right and I know I'm fairly predictable."

They went to a luncheonette around the corner. He'd suggested it; she said that's where she had in mind too. That little conversation before was a bit too sardonic or antagonistic, he thought; anyway, not good. They walked silently, darting looks at each other and smiling whenever they looked at each other the same time. That gave him a good feeling, and her suspicion seemed gone, if he hadn't just imagined it. They'd been to the place once before together, when it was way below freezing out and to warm up they ducked in for a bowl of soup they shared—vegetarian green pea with croutons in it—and tea and coffee. A roll came with it and she said the soup was very thick and the croutons too plentiful and she was already full so he eat it, and he said "No, I feel like I'm becoming a fatty these days," but by the time they left he'd picked at and eaten it all.

They sat at the counter, maybe, he thought, because that was where they sat the last time they were here. She just went up to it—all the stools were free—and he followed. No, of course the counter meant their stay here would be quicker than if they'd sat at a table. That wasn't a good sign—she didn't want to linger; just wanted to say what she came in to say and get out—or maybe he was wrong. If they were just here for coffee and tea, she wasn't the type, and knew he wasn't either, who'd take a table if the counter was available. But stop trying to make something out of the smallest things, for where was he after all these speculations: even. Whatever she wanted to say to him could be said as well at a table or counter and they could also linger here as much as at a table, maybe even longer because they wouldn't think they were taking up something as important to the luncheonette as a table for just a tea and coffee. If it was only a question of someone overhearing her, either the waitress passing or the counterman would. He thinks he has that right. "You want anything besides tea?" he said. "Sandwich, maybe; soup, piece of cake?" "No, I'm skipping lunch today." "Certainly not because you have to lose weight." Damn, now why'd he say that? "Thank you, but no," she said. "I had a big dinner last night so wanted to cut back on food today." "I remember you were very good at balancing out things like that. I wish I could have that kind of control over myself." "You did," she said, "and probably still do. You were always, as an example, eating light at night if you had a big lunch that day." "I did? Okay." They ordered coffee and tea. When the counterman went over to the coffee and hot water maker, he said "And can I have mine black please? And you want cream," he said to her, "right?" and she said "Milk." When they got their coffee and tea and her look turned serious and she seemed about to say something, he said "I was thinking. Oh, it's kind of a stupid odd thought, but I'll say it anyway, though quickly. We ordered and got tea with milk and a black coffee. But if I hadn't said make mine black, in so many words, and yours with milk, we would have got, if I remember right from the last time, black coffee with a little pitcher of milk on the side and a plain tea with a lemon wedge in the saucer, and you would have used my milk." "Yes?" and he said "This pertains to what we were talking about before—that 'shorter' business; cutting away verbal waste, though in this case actual physical waste too, since we even saved the place a lemon wedge which I also remember they automatically gave with tea if you didn't ask for milk. Only my one time in here but it really made an impression. Anyway, it was a silly thought, wasn't it, and now I'll shut up. What is it?" "What is what?" she said. "What we came in for and you wanted to tell me or talk to me about, I thought. I promise to be quiet from now on till you… well, you know, till you finish and maybe even after that, though don't count on it." She smiled, looked at the counter and her face turned serious, but a nice seriousness, a nice smile, nothing which indicated he talked like a bozo, a nonsense talker—his thoughts weren't coming out straight, and of course his speech neither, because he was nervous at what she was going to say. But a positive smile and an unthreatening seriousness, that was what he meant. One that was warm—the smile—and soft and so on. "I do want to speak to you," she said, "and about something I don't think you'll mind. I at least hope you don't. If you do, since it's been so pleasant with you so far, I'm sure we can work it out." She was going to say something good to him, he thought. That related to them both and the future of their relationship, he was almost sure of it. He got very hopeful. Felt, he could only put it, as if his heart had suddenly stopped. That sudden rush to it as if it were enlarging or expanding and exploding, or just one of those, or giving off little bursts. That was more it. Anyway, the heart. She was going to say she wanted to see him again, or if they could very slowly start over; something like that. Her look, the sense he got from it, and she now touched his knuckles, then slid her hand away, and now again the soft warm some-thing-good-coming smile. But looking directly at him while she made it, which she hadn't done in any way since he spot-ted her on the street, as if there was nothing to hide, they were going to be completely open to each other from now on. Everything pointed to all this; he couldn't just be imag-ining it. This is the way it can also happen. Thing with the other guy probably ended some time ago. Didn't know how to approach him—letter or phone—and then he was on the street, she thought it was an accident, or he convinced her it was, and she thought what a stroke of luck, she can tell him now. He won't say anything. Let her talk. Don't show any excitement, now or after she tells him, he thought. Show reserve, seriousness, nice soft smiles too, not giddy-like, because this was serious. This was their lives, maybe forever, the whole thing, who knows? So what could be more serious? "Are you sure you don't want some toast or an English muffin? I'll split it with you, meaning eat half." "No, I told you," she said a bit sharply, or just stiffly, though definitely not pleasantly, "but you have it if you want." "I didn't mean to be pushy, but I thought luncheonette, toast or English muffin; they go together. But that was silly, and you probably also don't have much time, and I said I'd shut up." He put his finger over his lips. She laughed, said "Talk all you want, not that I have to give you permission to. It's nice to hear you speaking lightly, kidding around, which is how I remember you, and without the edge and anger and then God knows what those last few times. And you're being nothing but solicitous to me, which I'd say was considerate of you after all we went through." What was that? Was there something she was saying but couching it in agreeable or digestible or pleasing or whatever the goddamn word for it is terms? He didn't know, or wasn't sure, but she was saying something that didn't fit in with what he was thinking before. "I'm sorry, what were you saying? I really didn't hear some of it because I was suddenly off into my own drifting thoughts." "About what?" she said, smiling. "Oh, drifting,

drifting, to be honest, some of it about you—your long beautiful blond hair. That's true, that's what it was, or close to it. The way it is now, worn down, but also worn up, worn any way, but not worn meaning worn-out, right? Sorry. Attempted joke." "And a good one," she said. "Good attempt, yeah, maybe that one, or just fair. But I loved being with you—that was also what I was thinking of then, or again, close to it, in my great drifting off. And, to be honest, I'm just about going crazy here sitting again talking to you. My heart—you can probably see it bubbling under my shirt—is literally going wild and might just jump out and grab you. Only kidding. But do you mind? I had to admit that. I couldn't just not say it. Not so much because of my sudden leaps of impulsiveness—and what the hell is impulsiveness but sudden? I can be so stupid sometimes—but because I didn't want to pass up this chance to tell you how I felt while you'd still listen. And you seemed to like being with me too. Not today, I'm saying, but months ago before I sort of cracked up over you. Of that, the way I acted, I'm truly sorry. But we never argued, never fought, never disagreed, almost. That all sounds boring but I loved it. You name it: shopping, talking, lovemaking, sitting in a movie theater, riding the subway, having dinner—whatever we did together I loved and seemed to go well. But I should probably just slap my mouth for bringing most of that up." "That's all very nice and sweet and touching," she said, "and relates to what I want to tell you and, as you said, we mainly came in here for." "I hope it's good." "What do you mean?" "Good for me, for you, for us especially, together. But it won't be, I'm afraid, will it. I've already blown it, haven't I.

Sincerity, honesty, spilling it all out, will get me nowhere. Nothing will. Being here with you, seeing you again—it was all intentional on my part, I have to tell you, or manipulated is a better word for it, once I delivered my manuscript. Only that part of the story was true. Ah, what am I even talking about there? I could have mailed it but thought if I delivered it personally I might bump in to you. First I went to your Grand Union, after the delivery, hoping you'd be there. Then Victorio's. If you were there—and what were the chances?—I even had planned what I was going to say. Something about biscotti. In the Grand Union, I forget; maybe something along the lines of what a terrific selection of cheeses they have, much better than any market in my neighborhood. But I'm just working myself up now, aren't I. If I stay a minute longer, hearing what you have to say, which I'm sure is 'I want to tell you how sorry I am for the pain I caused by breaking up with you,' and maybe also that you're tighter than ever with that other fella and he's moved in with you and you're even thinking of getting married and so on, I'll be a shell for the next few weeks, when most of that had recently ended. Now, just seeing you again, and if I can get out without hearing what you have to tell me, it'll last for maybe a week. You're so lovely, in every unfortunate way, what can I say? Nothing more, right?" She said nothing, seemed to be teary and biting her lip. Fixed a look on him, maybe to show how sad she was over it, then glanced at the counter and around the room, didn't know what to say and wanted to get away but also comfort him. "If something had to be said," he said, "something I'm not suspecting and which contradicts most everything I said, you'd say it, wouldn't you? Or did I, as I said, blow it when something good to my ears was coming? No, of course not. Do you mind paying? It isn't much and I really got to go. What an awful melodramatic finish. Well, they're all awful and talking about how awful they are is awful," and he stood up, turned around to face the door, was set to leave. She put her hand on his shoulder. So she was also standing now. Whatever you do, he thought, don't say any goddamn good-byes. Don't say anything, please, and he left.

He went home, hoping she'd be calling him when he got there. That she'd say she was going to tell him in the luncheonette, but didn't have the chance to because he talked a blue streak and then fled so fast, that she wishes they could see each other again or at least spend a single afternoon or evening together and see what happens. But that's the same dumb fantasy he had before he suddenly realized what she was about to say.

He was to meet a friend that night to see a play. But he called to cancel it, just so he'd be home if she did call. His friend said "You're wasting a good ticket for a supposedly great play which you already paid me good money for." "I'm not feeling well." "I know what it is," his friend said. "It's my stomach," he said. "No it isn't." "Ah, you're probably right. So what? So I got to go through these things the only way I know how. So it shows feeling. So it shows stupidity or something. Who's to say and what's the difference? I can see the play anytime and I'm sorry for disappointing you." "Don't worry."

MOTHER-IN-LAW

THEN, SHE'D COME down the stairs. One slow step at a time, holding the handrail because the stairs were steep and she'd usually be carrying something: a mug from the mug of tea she brought to her room the previous night or a towel or change of clothes or plastic bag of garbage or underwear she'd washed in the bathroom sink and hang up to dry on the clothesline outside. He'd be sitting at the kitchen table with his back to the stairs, drinking coffee and reading yesterday's newspaper or a book. He'd say to himself something like Damn, what's the big rush to get downstairs so early? No matter how early I get up, she's down here ten to fifteen minutes later. Soon everyone will be awake, she makes so much noise, or just my wife will, wanting me to exercise her legs and get her out of bed and give her medicines and so on, and there goes my morning solitude. He'd turn around and she'd be in her baby blue terrycloth bathrobe, which she'd leave in the hallway closet upstairs when she goes and he'd wash a few days before she arrived the next summer and hang on a peg in her room. Or he wouldn't turn around—he'd pretend he hadn't heard her—and she'd always say from the bottom of the stairs "Good morning," and he'd turn around, sometimes act startled, and say "Oh, I'm sorry, didn't know you were there; good morning," and she'd say "Did you sleep well?" and he'd say "Yes, and you?" and she'd say things like "Fine, thank you. The air up here; you don't know how lucky you are being away from the heat and humidity of the city. And it's so peaceful and quiet. Just silence or a bit of wind or a bird; no air conditioner. It's heaven." And then: "Is the bathroom free?" and he'd say it was. "I need to use it a short while, will that be all right?" and he'd say "Sure," or "Of course, use it for as long as you want," or "Feel free; I'm done and nobody else is awake yet," and she'd say "Thank you," and a few times "I hope I haven't disturbed you by coming down this early," and he'd say "No, why would you think that?" and she'd say "Your expression," or "Your voice," or "Some things I'm picking up; remember, my dear, I'm a psychotherapist," or he'd just say "Not at all."

Now, he's downstairs reading the newspaper. Morning coffee's being made in the electric coffeemaker. By the sound of it, it'll be done in less than a minute. He thinks: Wouldn't it be wonderful if she were here, coming downstairs now. Sure, her talking to him when he didn't want to talk to anyone so early or making tea and often letting the kettle whistle too long and also toast or the English muffins she preferred and boiling an egg and such interfered with his early morning routine. But she had every right to be here for the week or so she was—her daughter and granddaughters she adored and didn't see that much the rest of the year because they lived a few hours from her. And she was only getting her own morning routine going and to do so she had to come downstairs. A few times she said she'd been reading in bed the last hour or two—she'd mentioned the book; had he read it? No, he usually said, and would hold off saying but he had heard of it and is it any good— but didn't want to disturb the quiet of the house, perhaps even wake him and her daughter when she passed their first-floor bedroom on her way to the only bathroom in the house or just her shower running or her heavy old-lady footsteps, as she once put it, tramping downstairs. But why couldn't he have been more affable and gracious about the whole thing? Turned around when he heard her on the stairs and said "Good morning, how are you; sleep well?" but said it with a smile rather than some other kind of look he usually gave that early and which she was right in saying it was a dead giveaway how he really felt about her being down-stairs. And after she answered and then asked how he'd slept, said "Fine, thanks," and something about what the radio said the weather's going to be today and that the bath-room's free, by the way, if she wants to use it, and anything she needs for breakfast or her room and things like that, let him know. Would that have been too much; would she have seen through the fakery of it? Even if she had, and she cer-tainly would have wondered what was the reason for his change of disposition so early in the morning, she would have liked it a lot more than the way he typically acted, and probably would have said "Thank you very much; very sweet of you. But I don't want to be any more of a nuisance to you than just my being here already is, and I'm sure you have more than enough good things here for breakfast."

Then, he'd be sitting on the toilet, early morning, reading the newspaper, done a few quick exercises in the living
room and bathroom because he knew she'd be downstairs
pretty soon—done them fully clothed rather than just in
undershorts when she wasn't there—when she'd knock on
the door, or say behind it "Excuse me, is anyone in there?"
or turn the doorknob and slowly push the door open—there
was no lock or latch on it; still isn't and only way to keep
the door firmly closed without it opening on its own or the
wind from a downstairs window blowing it open is by slid-
ing a rock against it—and he'd push the door back and hold
it in place and say somewhat irritably "I'm in here; I'll be
out soon as I can." "Oh, sorry," she'd say, "I should have
knocked or asked before. Please take your time. Don't rush
on my account." Damn, he'd think, can't I even sit here a
couple of minutes without her wanting to use the bathroom? And what is she, so unconscious or oblivious this
early that she doesn't realize that, one, I'd be up at this hour
and if she didn't see me when she came downstairs it probably meant I was in the bathroom, and, two, if the bathroom door's shut or offers some resistance when she tries
opening it, someone must be inside? Maybe that's another
reason she should stay in bed and sleep longer: so she'll be
more alert when she comes downstairs. No, that's mean,
he'd think, stupid, mean, and truly overdoing it. But when
she does get in the bathroom she'll be there for half an hour
or more, showering, doing her hair and face, looking in the
mirror for long stretches, and possibly struggling on the
john, judging by the number of trips she makes to it and
the prune juice and mixed compote and lemon and hot

water she has throughout the day. And if he suddenly has to go to the bathroom again himself, which he does lots of mornings, no doubt because of all the alcohol he drinks at night, he'll have to go outside with some paper towels and a plastic bag for when he uses them and do it in the woods, which he had to do about every other morning when she was visiting them.

Now, he's sitting on the toilet, house is quiet, kids and wife are asleep or at least not stirring and his wife's not calling for him. No one to disturb him, he's saying, or interfere with his regular early morning routine, and it'll probably be like this for another hour. He can finish up here when he likes, sit on the toilet again in fifteen minutes if he has to, read there, in the kitchen, drink his coffee in peace, turn on the 9 a.m. weather report very low and maybe listen to the five-minute news roundup right after it, have another coffee and then the mug of miso soup he has every morning. Do all the exercises he wants in his undershorts and even without them, which he sometimes likes to do though always keeps his ears up in case one of the kids interrupts her sleep a minute to come downstairs to use the toilet. And then go for a short run through the mown fields around the house in his sneakers or bare feet and maybe only in his undershorts and a couple of times nude while holding his undershorts and come back and shower and house will still be quiet except maybe for the two cats meowing for food if he hasn't already fed them. But sitting on the toilet he thinks it would be wonderful, even here, if he heard her coming downstairs or already down them and approaching the bathroom. He'd distinguish her footsteps from the kids'. And if she knocked or said "Is anyone in there?" he'd say, well, he wouldn't say it irritably, that's for sure, "Yes, it's me," or "I'm sorry, I'm in here" and "but I'll be right out." She'd say what she usually said at the door, even the times she accidentally started to walk in: "Excuse me, please, don't rush for my sake," or a variation of that, "I can wait," and all very pleasantly. He'd get out quickly as he could, burn a match or two before he left to disguise the smell, which he always did when she or one of the kids was waiting to get in and he'd been on the john—kept, and still keeps, for that purpose a box of them deep in the back of a hard-to-reach bottom shelf; he's probably the only one who knows the box is there other than the landlady, who cleans the house before they arrive. Then he'd say, very nicely again—she'd be waiting in the kitchen or dining room (not the living room because, he's almost sure, it adjoined the bathroom and she didn't want him to think she could hear him in there), bathrobe buttoned up to her throat, hair in curlers with a kerchief over it, reading the part of yesterday's newspaper she hadn't read yet or a book she'd brought from her room— "It's all yours; sorry if I took too long." "You didn't," she'd probably say, or something like it. "You relinquished it much faster than I ever hoped for, thank you." So what's he saying with all this but that he misses her here this summer. Well, she wasn't here last summer either because she was recovering from a series of treatments for her illness and didn't feel her body could tolerate the trip, as she said. Misses her, period. She was so good with the kids, helpful to his wife, just a very kind and generous person who also pepped up the conversation when she was with them too.

She loved discussing all sorts of things she read in the paper, ideas she had on her own, books she recently read, movies and plays she'd seen, some of her crazier or more interesting clients, though never mentioning them by name or saying anything—especially about the ones in theater and writing—to make them identifiable or recognizable to his wife and him. Her early morning intrusions on his quiet? Looking back, what could he have been thinking of? He didn't handle it well, face it—should have been more tolerant, forbearing, obliging, the rest of that—and regrets it enormously. Oh, such phony words. But somewhere in there is how he really feels. He was a perfect shit most times, plain and simple.

Then, he awoke, looked at his watch by the bed, saw it was about quarter after six and thought Just get up now and you'll have the downstairs to yourself for the next hour. He dressed and when he left the room immediately got a whiff of her perfume or cologne she probably wouldn't have put on before her shower but which was stuck to her clothes or bathrobe from other days. Jesus, he said to himself, what's she trying to do, compete with him as to who gets up and around the house first? She knows he needs to be alone early in the morning, she knows it, at least for a few minutes! She's probably right now preparing or having her tea and prune juice or fruit compote and an English muffin, which she goes through a six-pack of every two days and where he can hardly keep up with supplying her them, and maybe even taken her exercise walk but not showered yet because that would wake him and then he might want to use the john. If she's in the kitchen or dining room he'll say good morning, get the coffee started, go into the bathroom and, once the coffee's made, excuse himself for a room she's not in, but be polite about it, for by offending her he offends his wife. She was sitting at the kitchen table reading the newspaper section he'd hoped to read with his first mug of coffee, tea, dish of cottage cheese, banana, slice of buttered toast in front of her, wet teabag in a jar lid she'll put by the stove and use for her next tea if he doesn't throw it out because when it dries up it looks so ugly, several bunched-up paper napkins and lots of opened sugar-substitute packs. What the hell does she do with that stuff, he thought, put it into everything she drinks and eats? He said good morning. Her back was to him and she gave no sign she'd heard. So he has to speak louder, he thought. Okay, it's important to her, these good-mornings, so be a good son-in-law and do it. "Good morning," he said a little louder. She turned around, startled. "Oh, you gave me a shock," she said. "You shouldn't tiptoe up on me like that. Give me a warning you're there. An old lady like me could get a stroke from such a surprise." "I'm sorry, and I didn't tiptoe up and I don't know how else I could have said good morning to you with your back to me. And it was the second time I said it; the first you didn't seem to hear." "I didn't hear because my hearing's going, which is nothing unordinary for someone my age. I should probably go in for a hearing aid." "I should probably too, but please speak lower. It's still very early, and the kids." "I'm not speaking loudly. I'm speaking normally." "Well, normally, in the morning," he said, "is just, I guess, a bit too loud. See how I'm almost whispering? Really, I think at his hour, that's how we both should speak, and that isn't a rebuke but an appeal." "My goodness, you certainly woke up on the wrong side of the bed. It's not what I need or am used to first thing in the morning." "I didn't wake up in a bad mood and I haven't got one now. I was only saying… but let's drop it. Did you sleep well?" "Yes, I did." "Is there anything I can get you before I start with my own stuff?" "No," she said, still angry. "I got everything myself, thank you, and need nothing from you." "Then if you don't mind— you know me in the morning: Mr. Solitude—I'm going to make myself coffee and read awhile on the porch. Unless you want to sit there." "Are you chasing me out of the kitchen?" "No, sit where you like, and please, please, your voice. It's… it's…" and with his fingers he said "Too loud." "Oh, you're impossible," and she got up and went outside through the porch. Damn, he did it again, he thought. Now he'll have to apologize and give some long explanation she won't believe. He should just keep his mouth shut with her in the morning, even when it's this early. Let her do what she wants, speak as loud as she likes. Kids are probably so deep asleep they'd never hear her anyway. But she should know better. Still, he should leave her alone, since it ends up like this too often. And for all he knows, maybe he is intentionally trying to rile her.

Now, making coffee, early in the morning, he thinks: What if she was right this moment coming downstairs? He'd turn to her immediately and say "Good morning; sleep well?" "Yes, thank you, and yourself?" "Fine, thanks, and it seems like it's going to be quite a nice day. Anything I can get for you?" "No, you're very kind, but I'll get everything myself, thank you." "Remember," he'd say, "feel completely free here. Anything we have and you want, take, and anything you need and we don't have, let me know and I'll buy it." "Kleenex," she used to say, day into almost every visit up here. "Why do I always forget to pack some with me?" and he'd say, though he doesn't think this or anything like it is what he ever said then, "And why do we always forget to have a box of tissues around for you? I'll get one today. Anything else?" "No. You can be very sweet when you want to, do you know that?" she once said about something else. Said a few times for different things he'd said and done. "Nope, never thought of it before and nobody's ever told me it either," he said once; "not even my wife." "You can be very funny too sometimes," she said. "You can really make me laugh when you're in a good mood and you want to get a rise out of me. I could never be that way, much as I'd love to make people laugh, which isn't to say I lack a sense of humor." "Well, needless to tell you of all people that I can be a pain in the poop too," he once said in regard to something else in another conversation. "But that's my nature, though I know I should try to change it." In fact he thinks he said it in a couple of different conversations with her and both times she answered in almost the same way: nature's extremely hard to change but not impossible, if that is deeply embedded in his nature as he says; just that it takes a lot more work than changing other things in oneself. "Sometimes one needs a therapist to help, though I know, because you've said so often enough, that you'd want no part of that." "True," he said that time or one of the other times she was referring to, "that right now and in the near future and maybe the distant one as well"—said something like this—"I wouldn't want to emaciate and emasculate most of my material, fraught with fraught or fraughtness as that statement might be, by meddling with or curing it, so long as I'm not really hurting someone like yourself or your daughter or my kids and so on."

Then, she was seated at the dining room table, staring out the window at the woods, or at least in that direction. Nothing was on the table except a pencil and large bowl of fruit they kept in the center of it. The pencil was new and sharpened to a point, one of the ones she'd brought with her to write notes in margins of books and a notebook. She did that every summer. She seemed to be thinking deeply about something. He didn't know if he should disturb her. But if he walked quietly around her she might get offended he didn't speak to her. She didn't seem to see him as he stood at the door between the living and dining rooms, though he'd think she'd be able to catch him out of the corner of her eye. He knew she was downstairs the moment he left his bedroom: her perfume or cologne. Or it's possible, he'd thought, she came downstairs for something—couldn't sleep so made tea and brought it upstairs, or used the bathroom and he didn't hear her pass his room or the toilet flush. He saw the bathroom door was open when he left the room, went in, washed up, shaved, did a few exercises in there and used the toilet, and then started for the kitchen to make himself coffee. She was in her bathrobe, the upper part open, exposing the top swelling of her breasts. She had large breasts, like her daughter, something he'd noticed before. Her hair was in curlers. She had a cloth of some kind around her head—not a kerchief but maybe a dishtowel—that seemed to be knotted under her jaw. Makes her look awful, he thought: curlers, cloth, her face shiny as if she'd put lots of cream on it earlier and hadn't rubbed all of it off. Or maybe she wasn't deep in thought. She could be sad or tired or hadn't slept well last night because of something she was thinking about for hours in bed or that was physically hurting her. A pain somewhere—she had arthritis in her hands—or another minor ailment or worse. Something neither he nor his wife knew about. "Good morning," he said. She turned her face slowly to him, smiled as if she'd just realized who'd spoken to her, and said good morning. She's going to ask if he slept well, he thought. "How did you sleep last night?" she said. She was speaking loudly and he wanted to say—after all, they were right below the stairs— "Please lower your voice; the kids upstairs," or just shush or put his finger over his lips and point upstairs with his other hand. But not this morning, he thought. Anyway, why bother, since she really has no control over her voice, it seems, after the first few seconds of correcting it. And he doesn't want to upset her again. For a therapist, she can be very touchy. "Fine," he said. "Slept well." "Man of few words in the morning," she said. "Right. Always have been, maybe always will." "Well I slept very well. It was almost cold last night. Great weather for sleeping." "That's why we come to Maine," he said. "It's delightful here. And the views, and that night sky. When it's clear and not so buggy do you go out every time to see it?" "I see it, or I've seen it; it's very pretty, very bright." "The two of you made the right decision renting this house and I benefit from it every summer, in addition to being with all my lovely dears."

"I'm glad you like it. It's very nice having you here." "Oh, stop," she said. "You know I'm a big bother and nuisance and that you simply put up with me half the time. And perhaps also because of the precedent of my visiting my daughter in Maine at other cottages long before she knew you. You both treat me too well, though. I feel like an overindulged guest at a very fine hotel sometimes, what with the delicious food you make and my lovely room and that you won't let me help you out with anything." "You're on vacation; just enjoy yourself." "And my hair," she said, touching the rag covering it. "You've been unusually tactful and well-behaved in not referring to it. I know I must look ridiculous with this getup. I'm also glad you didn't try to kiss me good morning with all this mush on my face." "It's true," he said. "I started to lean over to do it but was afraid I'd slip right off your cheek." "Very funny," she said, laughing. "You know, you can be quite the funny guy when you want to, and a very nice man too. I think I'm really beginning to appreciate you." "At last," he said. "It's only taken you fifteen years. Makes it hard not to try to kiss you after such a declaration. But if you'll permit me, because of the slippery cheek business, for now I'll resist." She laughed. "That a way to talk to your old mother-in-law? I'm only kidding, even if that wasn't one of your best lines. For the most part you not only can be very clever at times but have a fine use of words. I've always admired that in you. I kiss you, my darling," and she turned back to the window. "I don't want to disturb you," he said, "but like some tea? I'm going to make coffee now and I can always put some water up—" "No, thank you. I'm fine as I am." He went into the kitchen and pressed the coffeemaker switch. So what was that all about, he thought. Saying it just to make him feel good? Because she suddenly felt she had to for some reason? Or wants to get back to her own thoughts or thinks by making him feel better about her it'll help her daughter's marriage or just wants to increase her chances of having a peaceful week here? He doesn't do the same to her sometimes too? Everyone does it. We're all phonies that way to make things go smoother for ourselves; so what? But he knows she doesn't care for him or not that much. And why should she? He can be rude and argumentative, can get irritated at her too easily. While she, if she is angry at him, it's always, it seems, in reaction to something unpleasant he said, or a misinterpretation of what he said, but that's about it. So know that; make it sink in. But he's kidding himself, he thought, if he thinks that'll stop him from acting in a lousy way to her again. But who can tell? This morning—and he quickly looked back at her; she was gone, probably into the bathroom or living room, for she couldn't have gone upstairs or outside without him hearing her—they're off on the right foot thanks to her. Maybe it can continue. It'd be good for everyone concerned here, but it's all up to him.

Now, he sits at the kitchen table reading a book and sipping coffee. Last night he dreamt of her. She was sitting in a white plastic armchair like the cheap discolored one on the patio. One that he bought at Ames in town for ten bucks last year. She was staring at him, looked angry. He was standing a few feet in front of her and said "What's wrong?" She closed the book in her lap—she must have been reading before he came into the room, he thought—and continued to stare angrily at him. "Oh, I don't have to ask," he said. "It's the yogurt. You're still angry about the yogurt. Well don't let it stop you from reading." She didn't say anything, just stared. He has no idea what the yogurt part of it means. Same color as the chair, maybe? At least the plain yogurt he likes. Yogurt is aged, cultured, turned—something in that? She didn't like yogurt, he does. Anyway, his mother came into the room. She sat in the same kind of chair and smiled at him and said "Give it time, everything will be all right. I know what's going on and it'll be worked out." Then his mother-in-law smiled at him. The two women sat side by side in the same kind of chair smiling at him. His mother-in-law never said anything. "Good, I'm glad," he said to them. "I hate for there to be a continued disagreement over what appears to be a misunderstanding that can easily be worked out." So what does the dream mean? The two women are dead. His mother died three years ago. When his mother first came to him in his dreams—it was a couple of months after she died—she didn't speak either. She barely recognized him. At first, she didn't. He'd call her name— "Mom, Mom, it's me"—and cry in the dream, he once cried hysterically in one, and she'd keep looking elsewhere as if she didn't hear him and the few times she looked his way it was as if she didn't see him or was looking right through him or she was blind. This was the first dream he's had of his mother-in-law since she died four months ago. Killed herself. His wife said she hasn't dreamed of her yet and she wants to and he told her "Don't worry, you will. Then she'll come back fairly often, like my mother, I'm almost sure of it."

GO

SHE WANTS to go. Fine, let her. But he doesn't want her to. What does he want? Some time for himself, some easing of the work he does for her and all his other work, but he doesn't want her to go.

Why doesn't he want her to go? Ask yourself that, ask it, which he thinks he did but he'll do again: why? It has nothing to do with love. He isn't asking what it doesn't have to do with but what it does. But he wanted to get that in, that he loves her, though what the hell's love anyway? He means, what's love? A feeling, of course, though much more, but what? Love is…? Oh, what's he getting into, and he's losing this. Just snuff it and start from the top.

She wants to go, fine, let her, but does he want her to? No. Why not? Because he knows how he'll feel after. And that is? That he deserted her even though she was the one who left him. How's that? Because it was his actions that made her go. And he'd always be worried about her, would feel rotten he wasn't always there helping her when he could and as he has in the past, which was considerable. His help was. But he blows up too much because the work, all the work he does for her and also their kids and his job work and house and car chores and everything. It's work all the time, it seems, twelve to sixteen hours a day of it every day of the year or almost, so… what? Where was he? Talking of work and chores. His; endless, it seems. That he's conflicted about her going. He didn't say that but it has to have come out in what he said so far, and anyway, anyway, he is. If she left or let's just say was gone he'd have some time for himself. Now he has very little of it, so "some time" means more time than just a little. But he'd feel so guilty she left because of him and certainly couldn't have the help, she couldn't have it, he gives her and best of all when he gives it without bitching, that he'd… but he's forgotten again what he was talking about. It was… he was talking about… no, it's lost, or would just take too much to get back, so start again at the top.

She wants to go, fine, let her, but not "fine," because he doesn't want her to. All right: he does and he doesn't. He knows his life would be simpler in some ways with her gone, or just less tiring he'll say, a lot less tiring, and being taken care of by professional people: she would be. People whose profession is taking care of someone in his wife's condition. But he also knows it'll be tough for her in a way where it wouldn't be if he was around and taking care of her. It wouldn't be the same, in other words. Not as natural as him doing it, he's saying: paying strangers to look after her all the time. Sometimes they might get rough with her or pretend not to hear her when she called out from another room that she needed them. He always came when she called, which his what he meant by the word "natural."

That he was her husband, father of her kids, lived with her for many years, was in love with her all that time, so it was natural for him to respond whenever she needed him. Oh, maybe sometimes he took a few extra seconds to a minute or so to respond because he was in the middle of something—an interesting article or page of a novel he was reading, for instance, or involved in his own work—but no longer than that. Is that right? He thinks so. But he never got rough with her. Maybe one time he turned her over in bed a bit roughly and she hit her head on the night table. Actually, a few times, things like that. Lifted her off the toilet seat too roughly where she cut her foot on the wheelchair leg. Got her out of the front seat of the van too roughly where she banged her head on the door frame and got a big bump from it. But over the years, five to ten times he might have treated her roughly. Ten, he'll say, but no more than that, plus the ten or so times he was just careless in the way he handled her and she hurt herself. But he's talking of many years of taking care of her: around fifteen. Ten times in fifteen years that he was intentionally rough—that flipping her over in bed too hard where she hit her head; cut it quite deeply, in fact, that it took some time for him to stanch it and almost reached the point where he was going to take her to hospital Emergency—isn't that bad, he thinks, though of course no times would have been ideal. But he isn't infallible or a saint. He tries his best, or tries most times to do his best for her. Certainly he thinks he started out every time to do his best—no, that's not true. Sometimes he started out angrily to do something for her— was angry the moment she called out she needed him and he knew he'd have to stop what he was doing to take care of her—so of course the chance of an accident or him hurting her intentionally was greater than when he didn't start out angrily. So let's just say he tries most times to do his best for her. He asks her what the problem is or what she needs or he can do for her or knows or can see without asking and he does it, simple as that, or she just immediately tells him what she needs or wants done, though sometimes what he has to do for her is so hard or takes so much time that he gets angry while he's doing it and then becomes rough. He does have a little help in taking care of her, but only a little; he does most of it. "Only a little" because, for one thing, help can be pretty expensive. He also doesn't like these so-called professional homecare people in his house—"so-called" because some of them come close to being inept, another reason he sees a problem and even a danger in her going and relying on them exclusively. But anyway, he doesn't much care for them in his house, though of course he has to put up with it, especially when he's out, reading a newspaper or magazine or cheap novel or religious tract or pile of catalogs or just clipping out coupons from this and that, waiting for something to do for her. Waiting for her to call out to them from another room that she needs assistance, is what he's saying. And, as he said, or didn't say but is saying now, when he's in a relatively good mood, which is maybe two-thirds to three-quarters of the time—not a good-enough ratio, or whatever it is—percentage—but certainly not the worst either—he could… he means, these so-called professional homecare people can't help her as generously and willingly and naturally as he can. That thought could be straightened out. But the point is—well, lots of those thoughts could—but the point is—the one he was making or trying to make... what? Forgets. Thinks about it but can't bring it back. So just go to the start again, the top.

She wants to leave him. Fine, for her, he supposes, though he's doubtful about that, but not for him. Why can't she just accept that sometimes he gets angry at all he has to do for her and everything else but that he always realizes how wrong he is and apologizes for the awful things he's said, the threats that he can't take anymore of this and has to get out of here, that he needs a few weeks at least away from her and the kids and cats and all the chores he has to do around the house day and night. That he's sick and tired of it, literally tired and probably getting literally sick. But that he always comes around and does what he has to for her, meaning what she needs, and by "coming around" he means he eventually calms down and acquiesces and after that is always helpful and good to her and it's only rarely that he's in any way rough. But she's fed up with his periodic rages. She said—her actual words were—"I've had my fill of your crazy, dumb outbursts." That they're bad for her and the kids. That they might even make her physically sicker than she'd be without them. That he also embarrasses her when he flies into a rage in front of people outside the immediate family. And he knows he doesn't want to take care of her anymore, she said, so the best thing for her is to leave and get a small apartment in New York and someone there to take care of her permanently and he to stay in the house here with the kids and look after them, though for them to visit her often, she hopes, till they're grown and both in college.

But he said she'd need three professional homecare people to look after her; more than three. Three a day for eight-hour shifts and another two for two twelve-hour shifts on weekends, or however these things are worked out. At a minimum of twelve dollars an hour, for the year that'll come up to around... Well, figure it out yourself, he told her. How many hours in a week? Multiply that by twelve and then that figure by fifty-two. That's a fortune a year. Ninety to a hundred thousand. Maybe half of it paid for by the state or federal government, or both. But the other half they'd have to pay for, which means he alone, since she doesn't work. And that'll go on for years. Fine, let it, he wants her to be around for a normal life span and much longer. But that expense plus all the other expenses for her not covered by medical insurance and federal and state benefits will just about eat up every dime he earns. It'll eat up more than he earns when he also considers the cost of taking care of the kids for the next seven to ten years. College. How can he send them to college? How can he afford to continue making payments on the house? And New York. All right, she wants to be near her family and old close friends, but does she remember what apartments go for there? He'd have to get a second job to pay for it all. How can he do that and also see to the kids? So it doesn't make sense, her leaving. They have to stick together. He knows he's said too many times already that he'll change, but he will. He promises he won't go into any more rages with her and that from now on he'll take care of her with greater... how did he put it? With greater patience, consideration, and equanimity, he thinks, and without complaining, or with very little complaining. At least give him that, he said: the chance to complain a little, since he always goes back soon enough to acting affably or at least normally again. Because listen, he said to her in just about these very words, he hates the condition she's in, is distraught and depressed over it sometimes; that's not an excuse for his rages but just how he occasionally feels. But what gets to him also is all the work he has to do for her and all the other work he has to do at the same time. So what he's saying, he said, is that when it comes right down to it… what he's really getting to in all this… but he's stalling because he can't remember what followed it. Something to do with that they can't afford her living in New York by herself, meaning living there with professional homecare help sixteen to twenty-four hours a day. And "sixteen" because maybe she wouldn't need help between the time she's put in bed for the night and wakes up in the morning. No, of course she'll need someone there all the time. In case she has to use the bedpan or her leg falls through the bedrail or her feet get locked together where the pain's killing her and she needs them untwisted and straightened out. And to turn her, which he does at least twice a night, on her side or back so her muscles don't contract or go into spasms or whatever they do when they lie in the same position too long, but most importantly to prevent bedsores. So they have to stay together, if only because they can't afford to live apart. And for other reasons, of course. The kids; that overall he's the best one to help her; and he loves her, so naturally for that reason too he doesn't want them to split up. Though she has to know that sometimes all the work he does for her, and because he's far from being a young strong guy anymore, though he works out as much as he can to have the strength to do the more strenuous things, can be a bit too much for him, something he already mentioned but maybe needed repeating. What he hasn't said yet is that because of all this work, plus all the other things he has to do—kids, his job, etcetera—he has very little time to do the work that gives him a different kind of pleasure, if that's the right word for it—probably not—than helping her does. His creative work, he's saying. That's been his greatest frustration the last few years and what's led to or caused or is definitely partly to mainly responsible for all or most of his recent rages, he's almost sure of it, and maybe the rages the last few years too. He's no dope, though; he sees the conflict. Or "irony" or "paradox," he thinks would be closer to what he means. That even if they were able to afford her going because they suddenly came into a bundle or the federal and state social service agencies and his job's medical insurance plan kicked in 100 percent of her living-away costs, he'd feel so guilty that he probably wouldn't be able to do… he'd probably be able to do even less than he… he wouldn't be able to do even the little creative work he does now. He'd constantly be thinking of all the things she has to put up with every day because of her illness. The obstacles and frustrations, he's talking about, and that he wouldn't be there to help her over. That his rages forced her to go. That he knows he's the best homecare person for her overall because of his feelings for her and what she is to him and their kids and that he's not going to ignore her for more than a minute when she calls out to him or be anywhere near as rough on her physically as some of these homecare people have been. That she was probably getting used to living without him. It has its drawbacks, she'd think—separation from her kids, nobody much to talk to but the homecare people and medical personnel and physical therapists she goes to and a few friends and family when they come by or take her out somewhere—but she still finds that preferable to… well, there was a lot that was pretty good between them. The sex, which they continued to have, but not during the days of his rages; the meals he made and articles and pieces from books and newspapers he read to her; their talk about their kids and literature and movies they went to and other things and that he still always held her in bed at night, but even all that wasn't enough for her to endure his rages every week or more and anger about different things every other day or so. So… He's saying… But he's lost his flow of thought again. Lost the thought almost entirely again and whose voice he was trying to—or "perspective"—to speak through then. He could get some of it back if he ransacked his brain hard enough, but best to start from the top again, he supposes, and maybe this time around he'll coast right through.

She wants to leave but he won't let her. Meaning, he'll do what he can to stop her or, better, persuade her not to go. Convince her that it's in her best interest not to go: the kids, their mostly handicapped-accommodative house, not living with what are usually dull and often ignorant people all the time, that he wants her with him more than anything and will do anything to help her feel comfortable staying. For instance, changing his attitude somewhat and controlling his anger and other things, and what would those be? And changing his attitude how, and what's he mean, "some-what"? Well, just changing it, being easier about things, not letting them upset him so quickly and so much, doing… just doing… oh damn, he's lost it again. Had something, for a while it was lively, clear, and tight, but it got away from him. And as for "wanting her with him more than anything," he just wants her to stay, period; the rest should be obvious to her in everything else he says and his voice and expression and so on.

She wants to leave him and live in New York but he doesn't want her to and will do anything he can to persuade her to stay. If he has to—if nothing else he does works—he'll get down on his knees and beg her to stay. He means it. She must stay, he'll say. "I'm on my knees; that's how much I want you to. What else can I do to convince you?" But she must from time to time, he'll say, accept his futile rages against all the work he has to do and that his life is no life but really her life or mostly hers that he leads and though he realizes he's in a way fortunate… very fortunate to be in a position to help someone in her condition… to help her, and this is no baloney he's throwing either. He does feel fortunate he's able to take care of her… was put on this earth, almost, or just happened to be the person who was there to help make her life as normal as it can be under the circumstances. But it's also true that from time to time, as he said… Oh God, he's really messing it up this time—has messed it up, really, and right from the start, for noth-ing sharp and clear here. Everything was… let's just say he had a thought but let it run on and spill over to other thoughts till it was… what? Spilled, run over, making it impossible for him to get anything cohesive out of it. Just start from the top again but with a different tack.

She says she has to go. That there's no question of it anymore, she's going. When she said it, he said "Don't go; stay, please," and she said "There's no way that's possible," so he said "If not for me then just for the kids," and she said "Believe me, I've thought of that, but it's still impossible," so he said "Fine, then, go; it'll probably be better for us both and might make life easier for me, if you want me to be honest about it, though of course it'll be awful for the kids." But it won't be better for them both, he knows that. For the kids, it's awful when he rages and it'll be awful if she goes. What would be better, he can tell her, is that he adjusts to all the work he has to do now and which will no doubt become even harder in the future and tries to arrange things better, get professional help when he wants to do his creative work so he won't be frustrated he's not doing it, which would make things better for him and, in the long run, her, and, indirectly and also directly, their kids. But what the hell's he saying? And what's with this professional help, quote-unquote? Does he mean some kind of psychotherapy for him or just more homecare coverage for her, which they already have plenty of and is one of the reasons for his anger and rages? Not just the exorbitant cost of it they can barely afford, and let's say he didn't care about those costs anymore, or not as much as before, but that these people always seem to be in his way, cutting into his privacy, no time for him to walk around the house and think things out without bumping into them or seeing them out of the corner of his eye, and their generally being an interfering nuisance, for instance washing a single dish in the kitchen for a minute and blocking his way to the sink when all he wants is some water out of the tap to drink. But what's he going on about now with this, since of course "professional help" meant them and not possible psychotherapy for him, but he was only saying that the way he said it could be misinterpreted. He means that he knew what "professional help" alluded to when he said it, but the way he happened to put it could have been— Oh, forget it—it's lost, the thought is, whatever he was getting at, the one just now and almost everything from the top too.

She wants to leave him. That's what she says she wants. He says all right. Said it, he means. Then he said "No, what am I saying; you can't." She said "I'm sorry, but I've made up my mind. Believe me, it wasn't a hasty decision. I know I've said it before but this time I absolutely mean it." "You have said it before," he said, "and you've also said before 'and this time I really' or 'absolutely mean it' or 'plan to carry it out,' so why should either of us believe you're serious this time?" "Because this time is different. I've already—" and he cut her off with "Excuse me, I'm sorry for my sarcastic attitude just now. I apologize. It was totally wrong of me. Wrong attitude, words, and tone. Wrong everything, even my expression." "Thank you," she said. "I accept your apology, but it won't change my mind. And I want to continue with why I think this time is different. I've already begun making arrangements to go. I'm in touch with someone who will look after me in New York. A very competent live-in homecare person who is also a nurse. I also heard of the ideal apartment for me that will become available next month.

It's affordable, though I suppose we'll have to incur some financial sacrifices, and only needs minor renovation to make it completely accessible for me. I've talked this over with people whose judgment we both respect and they all agree it's a place I shouldn't pass up and a move I should definitely make. Even the kids reluctantly agreed that it's probably best I left, but because of their lives here and the size of my new apartment, they'd like to stay." He just stared at her, was heartsick over it, couldn't come up with anything to say. If he said "Have you seen this place?" what would be the difference? If he said… well, whatever he said, she was on her way. He had the same feeling in his stomach as when… but anyway, she said "I can't live with you anymore. It's obvious our marriage is finished. I don't want to make you feel even worse about it but my bad feelings to you and your overt and often demonstrated hatred of me and especially your violent rages are doing tremendous damage to the kids. Admit it, we'll all be much better off when you and I are split." "No we all won't," he said. She waited for him to say more, he shut his eyes and kept shaking his head, and she said "Believe me, we all will." "And I don't hate you," he said with his eyes still closed. "Not one bit, and no one can take better care of you than me." "Perhaps you believe that—the last part, anyway—but I…" and so on. She also said then that she does concede he can be considerate, helpful, and quite warm and congenial to her sometimes, but he always reverts back to, "and maybe this is too harsh a word for it but is the one that strikes my mind now," the monster he's become the past year and, before that, the demimonster the two years prior.

So there it is and this time he's almost sure he can't stop her. Words won't work, action neither, because what can he do, stand in her way so she can't get out the door? She'd call the cops—as a last resort. But first the kids would scream for him to let Mommy go if she wants to, "it's only fair and you can't force people to do things they don't want to," and he'd have to step aside. Even if he got down on his knees— of course he wouldn't, but even if he cried, pleaded, said things like—well, said anything; that he'd even "and this is no joke," see a shrink to try to work things out between them—all right, not a shrink but a psychotherapist, he'd say, a psychiatrist, whichever one she wanted him to go to, and work things out in himself, he means, because although she's the one who's sick, the problems in their marriage that came after it are all his, and by "sick" he means her physical illness—none of it would stop her from leaving him. He'll just have to get used to it. And be congenial and kind, not revert back to monster man, help her get her things together if she'll let him, even drive her to New York in their converted can and help her get set up. If she goes, it doesn't mean she won't come back. And certainly if the way he acts to her stays even, there'll be a better chance she'll come back. No, she goes, she's gone for good, he's almost sure of it. She'll see how much better life is without him. And in a year their older girl will be in college, and in four years, both girls. So one of the biggest reasons for them to resume living together would be gone. It's all his fault, he knows that, but there's nothing he can do about it. What's that supposed to mean? Just what it says, he thinks, or close to it. Maybe he can still stop her. Maybe it's only a matter of not having thought of every possibility to. By that he means… well, it's all there what he means, he's just too tired to put it in another way, just as he is with that last thing he said.

PAIN

HE HAS A pain, at first didn't pay much attention to it, thought it came from something he ate, then from too much coffee, or vodka or wine, or exercising, but it was almost always there, constant for hours sometimes, bothered him at night, he didn't tell his wife about it, but after a week of this and when he couldn't sleep and was turning over in bed a lot and had got up and taken something for the pain, she said "Anything wrong?" and he said no and she said "But you've been squirming around in bed," and he said "Oh, a slight pain in my stomach," and she said "Where, upper, lower?" and he said "Or maybe not even the stomach; the right side below the ribcage," and she said "You take anything for it?" and he said "So far nothing's worked; aspirin, ibuprofen, and just now some antacid liquid," and she said "So it's been going on for a while. How long?" and he said "It's nothing, it'll go away on its own," and she said "But how long have you had it? It's obvious, not just tonight," and he said "A few days," and she said "Does it ever let up?" and he said "A little," and she said "You should speak to Denkner," and he said "You know me; I hate seeing doctors except for my annual physical," and she said "Call him, just as a precaution, and he might even give you a simple explanation for it and solution over the phone," and he said "I'll see," but he didn't call and the pain seemed to diminish the next two days and disappear entirely for longer periods than before and he thought Good, it's going away, I wrenched something and now it's healing. I made the right decision not to call Denkner, because he would have asked me in for tests, wouldn't have found anything and the pain would eventually disappear, but the next night when his wife was asleep and he was reading in bed the pain returned worse than ever and so not to disturb her he took one of his pillows and got a quilt out of the linen closet and slept on the living room couch, or was able to sleep for about an hour because the pain at times was so great, and when he came back to the bedroom next morning to get his things his wife said "Where were you last night? I reached over several times and you weren't there," and he said "On the couch. I felt a little congested in the nose, couldn't sleep because of it and didn't want to disturb you," and she said "You take some cold medicine?" and he said "That stuff always gives me a pain in my penis later when I urinate, so I just don't trust it. But the cold, or whatever it was, seems better now," and his stomach pain, now that he thought of it, and "stomach" because about half the times the pain seemed to shoot across it and the other times seemed to stay in the same place right below the right side of the ribcage, was gone, but that day in class he nearly doubled over when the pain suddenly hit him and he told his students, all in their seats around the seminar table and some of them, he could tell, wanting to get up to help him, he was calling the break twenty minutes before he usually did because his stomach was upset but he'll be back the second half so nobody leave for the day, went to his office, sat in his reclining desk chair, closed his eyes and clutched his midsection and said "Pain, please go away, please go away," canceled the rest of the class and his office hours after and drove home and his younger daughter said when he walked in the door "Daddy's home early, Mommy," and she said "Yes, what's wrong, you look awful," and he said "Damn pain down there again but this one almost killing me; I gotta get in bed," and she said "Oh darn, you didn't call Denkner, did you, and I never reminded you," and he said "I forgot, or I didn't want to go, but please, I have to lie down," and she said "Listen, I know, lie down, I'll get you something for it; and it's probably nothing serious—we get ten scares for every real disorder—but you have to find out what's causing it," and he said "You crazy? Not right now," and went into the bedroom and lay on top of the covers, pain went away in an hour and he came back into the kitchen and said "Look at that; gone; I'm even smiling. I hope that's the last of it, for it was the worst pain I ever experienced, and I'm sorry for yelling at you," and she said "Don't get mad again but I made an appointment for you with Denkner tomorrow— 10 a.m., only slot he had open; I didn't even check with you if you were busy," and he said "I don't see why I should go. I feel fine, as good as ever, so only if the pain comes back," saw the doctor three days later, was examined, put through tests, couple of days after that the doctor called to say the lab results and sonograms indicate something quite serious could be wrong and he wants to refer him to a specialist, specialist said he had to be operated on soon as the hospital could fit him into its schedule, operation wasn't successful and treatments after that didn't work and he had to take a leave from teaching, he felt nauseous a lot from the medication, pain got worse, they had to hire people to take care of his wife almost all the time now because he was too weak to get her off and on the bed and other things, they were starting to be short of money, his medical leave ended and he had to retire and go on pension and Social Security, things got worse all around, he thought Damn life, everything's going okay, nothing great but he was at least able to move around freely and enjoy life a little and take care of things: his wife's illness, paying all the bills, his work at home and school and his writing and looking after the kids, and now nothing it seems but pain, weakness, and fatigue and everything else that's bad or comes with serious illness and he hates it, it's all so goddamn hopeless and he sometimes feels like doing away with himself but knows he can't because of what it'd do to his wife and kids and he's still able to help out at home a little so doesn't want to leave them completely in the lurch and also maybe some new drug will be discovered to relieve his condition somewhat, his doctors say researchers in various places around the world are working hard at it, so he has to hold on, nothing else he can do, got worse and more discouraged and depressed and almost every night after the woman who got his wife into bed had left and lights were out and they were in bed he thought of times before he was so sick, nights after he got his wife set for sleep, covers over her, he'd stand on her side of the bed and lean over to kiss her on the lips goodnight and every few nights would say, if they hadn't already done this soon after he got her from the wheelchair to the bed, "I know you're all set for sleep, but do you want to?" and his face would say what he meant and she almost always smiled and said something like "Sure, why not," or "I was hoping you'd suggest it, and if you didn't, I was going to," and they did it and then he got her ready for sleep again, shirt and booties back on if he had taken them off, head and shoulder on two pillows, bottom leg stretched out, doubled-over pillow between her knees, cushion between her feet, covers over her, kissed her on the lips goodnight, shut off her night table light, washed up and got in bed naked beside her, lay his handkerchief over his bed lamp so there'd be less light on her, make sure his watch, glasses, notebook, pen, and book he was reading at the time were on his night table, would read for about half an hour or till his eyes got tired and then would try to read some more even though it was usually late by now, he'd only get five hours' sleep, broken up by his having to turn his wife on her other side once or twice, before his younger daughter got up for school and he'd get out of bed ten minutes later, brush his teeth, wash, shave, and do calisthenics in his bathroom, pushups on his bedroom floor and dress and go into the kitchen and get food out for his daughter's breakfast and some things out for his wife's more elaborate breakfast later on, push the button of the coffeemaker which he'd prepared the night before, get the two newspapers from the driveway and sit and read the front page of one of them and drink coffee for about five minutes and then take a short run on the same streets almost every time, get back and start the van so the engine would be warmed up, take his pills which he had set out the previous night in a jar lid alongside one with his wife's, cut some fruit and put an English muffin or bread or a bagel in the toaster for his daughter and go out and turn the ignition off and she'd come into the kitchen around now and get her lunch ready and school stuff together and say "We should leave, I'll be late," and he'd spread cream cheese or butter on whatever he'd toasted for her and pour another coffee in a special mug that fits into the van's cup holder and she'd eat her breakfast and drink a glass of water in the front seat while he drove and sipped coffee and he'd say somewhere along the way "Main or side entrance or trailers?" and she'd tell him and he'd say "Pick you up at regular time today?" and she'd say yes or "Can I call you after school?" and sometimes she'd kiss him goodbye but mostly she'd just get out of the van and wave and from there he'd go to the Y nearby and work out in the weight room for about twenty minutes and quickly shower and feel great as he left the place and walked to the van and drive back the same route unless he needed gas and at home fill the kettle with water if he hadn't already filled it that morning or the previous night and put it on the stove and go into the bedroom and say as he pulled one of the curtains open "Time to get up," or "Ready to get up?" and she'd say something usually muffled under the covers over her face and if he didn't hear something like "A few more minutes" he'd open the big-window curtains but leave the other side-window curtains closed because that window was the only one his neighbors could see in and take his wife's covers off one by one and fold them and put them on a chair and remove her booties if she hadn't kicked them off at night and stick one inside the other and put them on the folded-up covers and take the rolled-up towel out from beside her back and pillow and cushion from between her knees and feet and put them on the same chair and get her on her back if she hadn't already managed to get on it and if she had, then straighten her body out, and exercise her feet and legs and then help her turn over on her stomach and she'd try to do pushups and stretch exercises while he went to the kitchen to turn the burner off under the kettle and prepare her soup, tea and liquid concoction she drank down the pills with every morning and go back and help her to her knees so he could get behind her on his knees and exercise her thighs, and sometimes, maybe once a week, more like every other, he'd pull down the pad she wore at night and say "All right?" and she usually said yes, and stroke her down there from behind and then try to penetrate her and sometimes, in anticipation of penetrating her after he exercised her from behind, he'd go into the bathroom and pee and put lubricant jelly on his penis, but coupling in that position almost never worked because he couldn't keep her steady enough to get his penis in, so he'd get her on her back and do it from on top or the side and then wheel her shower chair out of the bathroom to the side of the bed, lock the wheels, pull her by the ankles till her legs were over the side and then sit her up, make sure her feet weren't twisted and were flat on the floor, put his arms around her and say "At the count of three," and lift her onto the chair, straighten her up, buckle her in, unlock the wheels and pull the chair from behind into the bathroom, slide it over the toilet and take the bucket out from it, put a folding chair beside her, stick the pills into her mouth and hand her the liquid concoction, set the tea, soup, some fruit on the chair along with two slightly toasted rice cakes or lightly toasted rice bread with cream cheese or butter or egg salad on them, put her tape player by her feet with a tape already in it so she could listen to books on tape, go back to the kitchen and pour some of the kettle's boiled water into an extra-large mug with miso, grated ginger, and dried sea-weed in it, drink it while reading a newspaper for about fifteen minutes in the living room easy chair or, if it was warm out, on one of the plastic patio chairs outside, and then go back to the bathroom and pick up whatever dish she was done with and say "Everything all right" or "Okay?" and she'd say yes, or could he get her glasses and book or a certain numbered tape from the green Library of Congress or blue Princeton Recording for the Blind box on the bed in her study, one she's listening to is almost finished, and he'd do that and say "Anything else?" and she'd say no, "I'll yell for you when I need you," or "Just check in on me in half an hour," or "My portable phone," for he almost always forgot to give it to her when he gave her the rest of the stuff, and he'd get that and hand it to her or set it on the chair and close the bathroom door and sit at his table in the bedroom, put some paper in and begin to type.

BROTHER

WHEN— Among— Some twenty years after— His
mother— He was at his mother's apartment— He and his
mother were having dinner when— Out of the blue one day
his mother said to him— His mother called him on the
twentieth anniversary of— He got a phone call from his
mother twenty years after his father died and she said she
was going through her papers today— She said she was
rummaging through her papers the other day— She said she
was cleaning out one of her dresser drawers and found—
After his mother died he was given an envelope that had been
found among her— His brother came upon an envelope in
their mother's dresser drawer soon after she— Two weeks
after his mother died his brother gave him an envelope he'd
found in her top dresser drawer and which was addressed
to— A couple of weeks after his mother died he found an
envelope among her papers with his name on it and seemed
to be in his father's handwriting— And seemed to be his
father's writing. He says "seemed to be" because— After his
mother died, while his brother and he were going through
her papers— A week after his mother died he was given a

well-stuffed— A bulging regular-size letter envelope— He was given what's technically known as a number eleven— A few weeks after his mother died his brother and he— After his mother died his brother gave him an envelope with his name on it that he'd found in her dresser. It seemed to be his father's— After his mother died his brother gave him a letter envelope he'd found in her dresser. His name on the front of the envelope seemed to be written by his father, he thought. But he could be mistaken, as it had been twenty-five years—Jesus, could it really be that long?—since his father died, and maybe thirty to thirty-five years since he'd received anything addressed to him by his father, and opened it. His brother called him and said "I was going through some of Mom's things today and found an envelope addressed to you from Dad. I'm almost sure it's his handwriting. It's been so long—twenty-five years already, closer to twenty-six—that I could be forgetting what his writing looked like. I know it was a little sloppy and rushed, no dotted i's and few crossed t's and f's, and often illegible, nothing like Mom's. Remember hers? Clear, precise, somewhat ornate, almost calligraphic, as if she were practicing her perfect penmanship every time she wrote something, even the shopping lists she used to give me when she sent me out to shop. Dad was a lefty though, so that obviously had something to do with it, since he was forced to write with his right hand at school because his teachers—but you know the story. They felt left-handed writing was unnatural and threatened to hold him back if he didn't switch to right. He said they even used to pummel his left hand with a ruler whenever he wrote with it in class. Anyway, it's a regular letter envelope. A number eleven, I remember it was called when I worked in those offices Dad was always getting us jobs at when we were in high school, and sealed and pretty thick, almost bursting. Could be, after twenty-five-plus years, the contents inside need some air. It had your full name on it, and underneath in parentheses the words 'To be given—'" "It says on the address-side of the envelope 'Dear,' and I'm reading from it now, 'please give this to our younger son after my death. Nothing earth-shaking enclosed. I'm not assigning the family fortune to him. Thank you,' and then 'love.' So that can only be you, am I right?—if this is from Dad. The 'younger son'—since there are only two of us and I distinctly recall the day you were born. You know the story. After being toilet-trained at an exceptionally early age more than three years before, I suddenly, right after I heard about your birth, and worse, that you were a boy, began peeing in my pants and bed again for a week. I no doubt saw you as a serious contender to my—ah, what am I doing? Trying to say something clever about dauphins and childdom, but that would've been inaccurate since the eldest son of a—anyway, I gotta get going. I'll mail you the envelope first thing tomorrow," and he said "Don't bother. I'm coming in this weekend to help you dispose of Mom's things and also have a last look at our old place before we give it up, so I'll get it then."

He met his brother that Saturday in his mother's apartment, which was where they grew up, and after they'd separated a lot— They met that Saturday in their mother's apartment. After they sorted a lot of her things into stuff they'll— After they'd separated a lot of her belongings into things they'd throw out, things they'd give away and things they'd divide among them and their sister in California, his brother said "Oh, the envelope; I forgot about it," and went into their parents' old bedroom and got it. "I discovered it in her bottom dresser drawer along with a slew of useless documents and Christmas and Hanukkah cards and announcements of every kind, births, weddings, baby showers, some of them going fifty years back. You ought to look at them before I throw them out. Did you know she was such a hoarder? I always thought of Dad as the one who saved every little thing. Nothing sentimental like Mom's things, though. Used shoelaces and barely reusable envelopes and broken pencils and what I sort of found unpleasant in a different category of saving, for the lunch he brought to work every day the same greasy brown bag till it was in tatters and wax paper for the sandwich till it couldn't even be salvaged with a rubberband around it. And rubberbands and paperclips too, some of which you had to bend back in place to use, and you know how far that got you. While Mom would throw things out indiscriminately, it seemed. One day my Lionel train set I hadn't used for a few years was in the trash can outside." "You're talking about my train set," he said; "that happened to me." "No, I know it was mine and maybe I just loaned it to you after I'd stopped playing with it. But I never intended to give it away for good. I wanted, later in life—like about thirty years ago—to pass it down to my kids. Anyway, I also found several Indian pennies and silver dollars from the late 1800's in the same drawer, which we'll divvy up or you and

Sis can have them all. Am I right, though? It's Dad's hand-writing?" and he said "Looks it. What his teachers managed to do was beat it into an instantly identifiable individual scrawl. But this is amazing, something from the past like this," carefully opening the envelope and seeing it was a let-ter to him ("My dear Juneyboy," his father's nickname for him, "Juney" for junior and the month he was born), and turning to the last page seeing the words "love dad." "It's him, all right. Same sign-off and punctuation of it and everything," and turned back to the first page. "I know the year, but what day did he die, May 3rd?" and his brother said "Thereabouts, but for sure, May. We both stood in front of his gravestone not so long ago, so how'd at least one of us not mentally record it? I guess we were too busy, or what-ever you want to call it, with Mom." "So written approxi-mately a month before he died. How'd he get the strength? He was so sick then." "The last couple of months he had a few good days, or days a bit better than the miserable ones he usually had, and how much strength does it take to write a letter? Though that's quite a long one, so maybe it took several days, and possibly some of the last good ones left to him." "What the heck could he be saying in it? You didn't find any similar letters to you and Sis in that dresser?" and his brother said I went through both dressers and every drawer, box, shelf, closet and pocket and book and shoe and sock and such, not to look for a letter from Dad to me as much as that I didn't want to leave anything… well, to be thorough, that's all. Forgot to tell you I found a fifty dollar bill in an otherwise empty envelope with nobody's name on it, which'll go into the entire estate, but nothing else like that. Nope—you're it. And you're obviously curious about the letter, so take a break and read it now." "I think I will," and he went into the kitchen and made coffee, yelled out "I made a fresh pot of coffee, want some?" and his brother said "I've been told to lay off anything caffeinated, and Mom never had any other kind, if I'm right you're using hers. By the way, you see something in the letter you think I might be interested in, let me know," and he said "Listen, you can read the whole thing after I'm done with it," and his brother said "No, too much like snooping, and I'd also break down, I think, hearing Dad's voice after so many years. I've got a ton of his letters from when I was in the army and before that, in summer camp and college, and I haven't reread one of them since he died. With yours, just paraphrase for me the more pertinent impersonal passages— The pertinent impersonal parts— Just give me the juicier non-sad highlights— Just highlight the passages you think I'd be— Highlight the parts you think will interest me," and he said "If I can remember them," and sat down at the kitchen table with the letter and a mug of coffee and started to read.

"This might come as a huge surprise to you," his father wrote, "getting a letter from me through Mom. But it's what I asked her to do after I die, give it to you. Because you're a writer I thought you would like to know something about me that hadn't crossed the dinner table, as we used to say ages ago when I was years younger than you are today. You've been writing without letup for years from what I could hear from your room when you were living here. And by what your mother tells me, because you never give me a straight answer anymore, that hasn't changed even though you've had no success at it. So who knows if you haven't run out of things to say, or for now, or the things you write about just don't bring you much attention or any money, and that I'm not wrong in thinking what I got here to tell you about myself can be of use to you. Because I have had an interesting life I think. Rags to not so much riches but just a hell of a lot better than what my folks had and gave me and plenty of bumps and a few big ditches I fell into along the way. So lots of changes in it I'm saying and more than enough excitement and heartaches and plenty of characters. And characters you once told me—you see? I don't forget every word you say ten seconds after you say them as you once accused me of—are for what make good fictions. 'Without interesting characters and situations and the changes coming from them,' you said, and something else, a lot else. But anyway even if I can't repeat the exact words in total I do remember the crux of it and that could even be more important than quoting somebody like a tape recorder. And maybe some of my life can be put into your own written words and sell. That wouldn't be such a catastrophe. You could always use a little more money to live on and maybe even a lot more if you do want to marry and have children as you've professed, which is my five dollar word for this paragraph. And even though you said over and over till it became a headache to hear anymore how the last thing you write for is money, if some came your way with your name on it you wouldn't turn it back, am I right?

"But enough with the introduction. Way I'm going I'll be dead and buried before I have a chance to tell you anything about my life. And excuse me in all this for my occasional cynical note and joke on you. Because believe me it's all in good fun and I don't mean to hurt with it. And the last worst joke is on me anyway, since you're reading this soon after I probably moaned in pain till they got rid of it while they also got rid of me. And also excuse me for my poor English and punctuation. You can always fix that up for me if you don't want to leave it as is, which might be more real for someone to read than you polish it up and redoing it and such till it's perfect. But it's all yours what I'm going to say here and you do with it what you wish. I'm not for sure going to get angry at you from heaven or wherever I end up. Heaven would be nice because there I'd be with my mother and father. And not being much of a reader except of newspapers and occasionally a business magazine and one or two times an overcomplicated detective novel when I was stuck in a hicktown bus station or a resort without a newspaper, I shouldn't be telling you your job. But if you've had no luck at it after trying for about fifteen years maybe doing it another way and with different ideas than yours sprinkled in it will change things to the better for you. So let's get to my life business. Though maybe I should put it off till later and with no five dollar word in this paragraph like the other ones. For suddenly I feel—actually here it is at the finish line but you'll probably think it lightweight—tuckered out.

"So I'm back, my juneyboy, rested and feeling better, but where to resume? I already said I figure some of this could be useful to you. Or I think I said that since I didn't read what I wrote back and I barely have a newly happened memory. Things from the past though I'm great at. There could even be lots of articles in this for you which I think will take me a few days to compose. Compose? How do you like the words I'm using and you never heard from my mouth. I think— I should say I don't think I ever used that word before in any way but music. Gershwin composed this, Irving Berlin composed that, Rakmaninof, and don't expect me to spell that right or know what his first name is, composed a piano concerto probably. But they all composed I'm saying. Not that I know the titles to anything they did compose but 'White Christmas.' And 'Rhapsody in Blue' because your mother and I saw the movie on its opening night at Radio City or the Roxy for some benefit. But I'd hear the music on the radio and the announcer would say 'By George Gershwin' or 'The second sonata by whatever his first name is Rakmaninof.' Then I'd forget who wrote the piece till the next time it was on the radio and a different announcer would say what it is and by who. But it must be the act of writing that's making me use words like 'compose' in the way I did. That's what people who aren't real writers do, start getting elaborate with their words and which is another one I never heard myself speak, 'elaborate.' So I'll try to contain these words so they don't stand out and look unnatural to what I'm writing. Also it isn't as I said that I've a whole decade left to get everything in my head down. But time to rest again. Who'd think that just scribbling with a pen could be so tiring? Possibly because I know I've such lousy handwriting so I'm trying extra careful to make it easy for you to read. In something like this I'd think you'd want to understand every word. I'll be back.

"Certain things in my childhood I like talking about

you mostly heard too many times so I should probably skip them. That business of sleeping on my family's apartment fire escape when it got too hot inside. Also in summers walking around in torn shoes and sometimes bare feet to save on shoe leather of my one good pair for the fall. Starting to contribute money to my family when I was eight and never stopping working all through school and after that till sick old age. My mother who I worshipped and you never knew because you were named after her and so on. Even if I hadn't told you everything about my life then who'd really be interested in things of someone so young? Adults want to read about adults would be my guess and you don't write children's books. My father who you also never knew and your brother's named after who was such a good-hearted softie that my mother walked all over him. I swore to myself early never to be like that. I think I succeeded too. I wasn't ever a hard guy or a mean type I don't think but I was also never a pushover even when I got this sick. I stood up for myself and pushed people in a boy-from-the-boys' con-genial way to make a better life for me and I think that's why I got the success I did. You should be more like me but you never will. I tried to teach you without saying any-thing, mainly since I didn't think you'd ever listen to my advice, or just saying enough but none of it worked. Your mother's much more the influence on you because the weak way you act and accept things and often let yourself be a doormat for is like all the men in her family except her father and including her brothers-in-law. That's why I think your mom's father and I got along so well. He saw in me— But what's the point talking about it. You did get some of my stubbornness though. But maybe only with me since you let every woman you dated who I knew run you to the ground when most of them weren't worth being with to begin with. All with no looks and little personality and coming up short in the brains department also which you'd think they'd have to make up for the other things. You were always too nice to them, polite, doing this for them, that. Going out of your way for them, overboard it seemed, maybe just to get them in bed or keep them there if you already made them. But you lose too much of yourself doing that. They should come to you because of your strength and unwillingness to bend and the kind of work you do and having some money helps. Sure, be good, never rough, and occasionally you have to give in, but you don't want to be a complete patsy. But I don't want to labor that point either. This is supposed to be about me, stories for you. And me without what I think of things or any philosophy but just the action and circumstances of the events so you can write about them. And all these incidents with your own women you probably wrote about and they didn't sell. Because who wants to read about a nice softie who gives up almost every part of himself just to have a plain woman with no spark in her on his arm? For myself I always wanted to be a man first, then a husband and father. For without the first you can't be too successful at the others. So what else can I tell you that will be of anything interesting? I suppose I should put in I did some wrong and embarrassing things when I was no longer so young that I could explain them on that. Stuff I'm not ashamed of I'm not ashamed to admit since they're over and done with for years and that was always my attitude anyway. Not to dwell on past wrongs and shake my poor head over it since that can only stop you from thinking good things about yourself and getting ahead. Although these weren't things I did that I ever wanted to see in print you know. Now I don't even care about that since I'll be gone when you read this of course unless by some mistake where you get it before then and I only hope you make lots of bucks off of it. But what these embarrassing things were and which I think would be interesting for you to write about I suddenly forget. We were poor. The neighborhood was rough. Plenty of real criminals, most who ended up in prison or who didn't die of old age. I might have done some things illegal too. But that was when I was very young and not the time I'm referring to you about. I know I never did anything drastic. Nobody or anything hurt in a physical way because of me but I still can't remember what they were. I always had to work for a living. I know I told you that in this and a thousand times before. I gave my mother most of what I earned as a boy. Even as a grown man I was the main one to support my folks till they died. When my mother died you could say that for me it was like a parent losing a child. My father I didn't hand over money straight to because he liked to drink so only to my mother. I didn't have a bad life as a kid but I had a lot more fun when I was grown. I knew lots of dames before I married. That's no secret to your mother and she even said she's glad I got that out of my system. Since marrying her you could say I've behaved like a saint. I haven't but you can say it. I'm only joking there and I don't know why I'm reeling off all these little things when I said I was going to concentrate on stories that happened. No doubt I'm hoping a specific incident will jump into my head from one of those that I can then relate. But none has and I'm tired now suddenly so I'll nap a while and come back later or tomorrow.

"So I'm back the next day and we'll scrap my big-word-in-every-paragraph routine and wondering if this letter that's supposed to be useful to you is a true picture of me. Or have I said that in it? Reading the last paragraph back I realize that giving dough to the family from your wages as a kid wasn't anything you ever did. You kept everything you earned then and of course later as a man. I suppose you felt I made and saved enough to keep things going for your mom and me so you didn't have to pitch in. You were probably right because it's true we lived well enough and were never short of cash. But at the time, mainly when you were a man, I felt you could have forked over some to your mother. Mostly as a gesture of some kind on your part and also just in case something happened to me much earlier than it did and she'd end up needing every nickel she could get to supplement her Social Security and the savings I had put in. Your brother always volunteered a little as a kid but when he got married and had children so early I didn't expect anything more from him. I guess I also wanted

"I'm back again after a break of another day. I suddenly got so tired writing that I couldn't even finish that last sentence yesterday. What I was going to say there I forget so I'll leave it at the end blank. So, my youth was concerned mainly with school and work after and learning how to live on and off the street. My three educations I called it. The other stuff—the crowded Lower East Side where I grew up, what life was like then and people did, two for a nickel movie tickets, clothes, food, freezing tenements, the first cars in the streets and even the last of the horsedrawn trolleys if I'm not remembering that fact from movies and old newsreels—all of it you can get out of the history books or by just walking up the block to the New York Historical Society Museum we have here. (Now that I think of it living almost next door to that museum and the American Natural History one should have given you two free educations but you didn't seem to make much use of them. I know your brother did and I would have as a kid.) So what I'd like better to get down here is what life was like for me and some of the more interesting characters and incidents. For that's all that good storytelling is, isn't that right? But you tell me, you're the expert—and maybe you have and maybe I've already said all that also—for what do I know? Damn I'm getting tired again—*getting tired* is a joke; I'm always tired, just sometimes I'm dead tired—so again I'll have to stop. Nothing's coming into my head anyway now about what I want to write. Maybe tomorrow and all the following days till I've lots of stories down. How I met your mother for instance. That's a good one and adult. You probably think you heard it all. But that one your mother and I tossed over the table was just for the amusement of you kids. The real story will be an eye-opener for you and is something your mother who knows I'm writing this letter has given me the go-ahead to reveal. Another eye-opener will be what I did for a living in my late teens and early twenties long before I met her. If I said in this I've never done anything illegal but in my young youth that would have been untrue. I know you think I went right from high school into dental school and a legit practice, but there was a three-year stint in between where I did some frankly questionable things and paid for it. For a while after I married I regretted them. After that I just forgot about it or would never mention it in front of you kids because I thought you'd be ashamed of what I did. I could take that, what you kids thought of me didn't phase me much, but I didn't see the point in giving you ammunition to think even less of me. For the last few years when I look back I think hell, at least I took chances with my life and had some excitement and adventures and fun and even made a bit of dough off it. While most guys their whole lives live like gutless dullards and think they're so good and aboveboard because of it. But all that for later and which I thzink are the real stories of mine you'd want to use. What I'm also thinking is that if I do suddenly get hit by a fatal lightning bolt between my nap now and tomorrow I should get a couple things down first and not just to make you feel good either. Let's face it we rarely saw eye to eye on things once you got to be fourteen or so. We had our differences and some terrific arguments over them. They for the most part consisted of you screaming your red face off at some viewpoint I'd taken and wouldn't change my mind over and me just sitting there thinking and then forced to say that you were such a nice kid once but something happened where you became a total misfit, nutcase, and hysteric. Despite all that you have to admit I never once hit you with anything harder than a fluffy bath towel a few times or punished you much for your fresh mouth. Maybe ordered you to your room which you either went to or you didn't or asked you to leave the dinner table because you were ruining my appetite and by that time you wanted to go anyway. But I mostly deep down respected you for your strong convictions and standing up to me, but as I said I only wished I wasn't the only one you did that to. The truth is I liked you your whole life long despite our disputes and your rude and often foul-mouthed behavior toward me. And that when you were a kid I loved you tremendously even if I didn't show it with much attention and doing things with you or your brother and sister, though maybe a little more with him because he was the first child and new for me and he didn't have you to play with yet. Though I had my own concerns. I was busy making money for the family and dealing with matters outside that had nothing to do with children, so I felt I couldn't afford the time. I now see that as a big mistake and I'm sorry. I should have been doing things like taking you to baseball games, teaching you baseball, not that I would have known a throw from a catch. Sports didn't interest me except professional boxing which you hated. Too violent for you and one of our arguments I now remember if not many of them. I wanted to take you to a couple fights but knew you'd want to go home before the main bouts. I just should have done it and not thought of myself. Who knows, maybe you would have got excited like I did at them and seen the skills involved and changed your mind. But more truth is that I probably loved you almost as much when you were grown up except for those times you went at me with your mouth. But even there as I said I admired your spunk. I just never thought to put what I felt for you in any way but smiles and jokes and buying you things like the liverwurst you loved and stroking your hair and such. Ask your mother what I thought of you. I know I told her a lot how I felt about you kids. But you especially. When it comes down to it you were my favorite. Maybe because you were the only one who idolized me when you were young and did most of the things I asked you to your first fourteen years. And like me you usually had a job from early on and hardly ever any lip from you. You were the one I pinned my greatest hopes on in what you'd do with your life and type of guy you'd become. Your mother told me lots of times to tell each of you kids how well I felt about you all. But not the part of course that I felt especially close to you because that would hurt the others. To not even tell you that because it could get back to them. I told her it just wasn't in me to make these kinds of confessions to my kids. At the time I thought it wouldn't be manly to tell you boys how I felt like that and it would seem wrong in a peculiar way to tell your sister. I wanted it to be done by what came out from how I acted but I guess I did a poor job of that. I also thought she told each of you individually how I felt toward you kids. But when I asked her about it not too far back she said she never spoke to any of you about this because I thought I'd say something but it never came out. I just sat there like a statue or talking nothing really when what I wanted to say was that you were always my favorite but never tell the others. That I loved you dearly almost every day of your life and was sorry I hadn't told you before. I didn't want to make you feel bad but just wanted to once and for all get everything out. I was also going to say that matter about my greatest hopes and because of it my biggest disappointment. I mean of you taking up what you did for a living and sticking with it when it was obviously a hopeless situation and not going into something else while you still had the time and which I would have helped you out with in tuition if it took more schooling. But that it's all okay for me now because I've accepted it. That it's your life and so in a way I have to admire that you went and stayed with what you wanted and didn't listen to me about it. And also that I know I did more things wrong than right for you and practically the reverse from you to me, so you're way ahead of me, way ahead. It was probably too late anyway. All the damage from my side had been done so why would I think at the last minute I could undo anything that my death won't? And the last few days or whenever I first came up with the idea I thought it best to just put all of it in a letter and not a speech or in a phone call. Also looking back now that I'm sick and old and tired all the time it seems and no longer working for years I regret I let my work dominate my life so and that I didn't, which I said already but maybe needs more saying, put in more time with you kids. But as I said I wanted to get this down in case tomorrow a trolley car—but they don't have them anymore so a bus flattens me when I'm being wheeled around outside or that lightning bolt from nowhere I spoke of. But where'd all the stories I was supposed to tell you go? I meant to put them in and not yak so much about my personal feelings. I'll save them for a second letter sometime later. I'm telling you, some of them you'll find very useful. But this one just to be safe I'll close now and stick in an envelope if I can find one in this place and seal up and give to your mother for you," and signed it "love dad." And underneath that: "P.S. (as if you haven't had enough of me already). To be completely frank as your mother likes to say what I intended on doing when I started out with this was only to give you a few good stories of mine. But I got sidetracked with the other stuff no matter what excuses I gave for writing about it. I'm glad though I at last got what I've for a long time wanted to say to you out even if it had to come at the expense of—well, something but I forget what it was. Probably wasn't important. love dad."

He didn't know why his mother hadn't given him the letter. It was sealed so he thinks she never opened or read it. What's he talking about?—of course she wouldn't read it. She never did anything like that. If she'd wanted to know what was in it she would have asked him and if she'd wanted to read it he would have given it to her. She intentionally stuck it in her dresser drawer along with other papers. Or wherever she put it first but it ended up in that drawer. He went into the living room. His brother was folding pillowcases to put in a big carton and he said "Which dresser did you find the envelope, Mom's or Dad's?" and his brother said "Dad's old one which became Mom's second dresser after he died, why?" and he said "Just curious; no real reason. Or my innate predilection, or professional obsession if you want to call it that for... ah, forget it. You're right, it's silly," and his brother said "I didn't say that. It's funny, though. There's nothing of her linens or clothes, and she had some fairly nice things—a mink stole, even—I or my family want. And Sis says the same: get rid of everything, and the stuff you can't sell give to Goodwill or put it on the street. And it was just about the same with Dad. She only wanted a pair of cufflinks, you took a tie, I think, and I got an old cummerbund and brand-new tux suspenders I've never used, though I know where they are. Everything else went to that Christian residence house down the block that took clothes and such for missionaries on their way to Africa. We should find out if they still take those things." "I'll check. By the way, you didn't find another envelope or something like that from Dad to me?" and his brother said "Hey, one's not enough? And such a thick letter? You're the special guy, the child of choice," and he said "What are you talking about? One of the great things about Mom and Dad was that they played no favorites. And you had them alone till I was born, so if anyone was special for a while, you were. And then for a couple of years, Sis, after you and I moved out. Me? The typical middle kid, with neither parent paying that much attention to him," and his brother said "Oh, yeah; anyway, I was only kidding. So, anything interesting in the letter? I'd think so," and he said "Nothing, really. Things about what he wished... I mean that he wished... he had hopes for many years that I'd take his advice and go into a different more lucrative profession than the crazy undependable one I chose, he said. And that he didn't see how what I was doing with my life—no steady job, girl here and there—was going to help me get a nice wife and kids I could afford to have and a comfortable place to live—something like what your brother has, he said—and so on... You know, that was twenty-five years ago. And that he'd always thought, though I don't know where he got this from, that I had a good head for the sciences and how he would have helped me though medical or dental school if I'd've taken all the pre-med courses for it and got in. But that he had finally adjusted to it. Mainly because by now, meaning then, he knew I was getting a bit too old to return to college to take the required science courses needed to apply to med or dental school and that my mind was probably made up anyway on what I wanted and didn't want to do with my life. But all said very calmly; Dad making peace with himself over his one unfortunate son." "Oh, get out of here." "He also said he was writing a letter to you and Sis, which I suppose meant individual letters, but you haven't found any," and his brother said "I looked high and low and then some because I thought there might be once I found yours. Could be I haven't explored a few places, so they could still turn up. But is that it?" and he said "With the letter?" and his brother said "Sure, it was so long." "Ah, lots of stories of his we're both pretty familiar with, he told them so much. You know, how he and Mom first met at an Al Jolson show on Broadway. She was with her brother and Dad knew him because they'd once worked in the same building. And how he thought they'd hit it off right away but she later told him when he called her—" and his brother said "It's okay, I remember. But he called? I thought the story goes where he went over to where she lived with her family, which was only a few blocks from him, and knocked on the door." "He said 'called.' And that business about his family being so poor that in the summer he had to walk around barefoot to save on the—" and his brother said "That was a joke, you didn't know? Like the one he told where the bedroom he and his siblings slept in was so small that the furniture was painted on the walls. The family was definitely poor, though." "The shoe-leather story was a joke? I always believed it. I even told my kids it. Why would he repeat it in detail to me as if it really happened?" and his brother said "Don't ask me. Maybe he got a kick out of continuing to fool you. Just think of the laughs he would still have if he had lived till now and continued to tell you the story. Because listen, if it were true, how would he have held a summer job as a boy? Since he also used to tell us, and this story I'm sure was so, that he worked full-time every summer since he was ten, compared to how he did it the rest of the year, which was to work only on Sundays and after school." "You're right; what a gullible schmuck I've been. For in this letter he also brought up several of the jobs he had as a boy, and I have to assume some were in the summer and would have taken shoes or something other than just socks on his feet. Runner for a bookie." "That one I never heard." "Yeah, that's what he wrote. Even thought seriously, when he was around eighteen, and no doubt because of his early experiences at it, of going into it as an adult. Also, delivery boy for a button and then a belt company. And how when he was given trolley fare for some deliveries he'd walk or run them instead and pocket the money." "That one I remember. I used to do the same thing when I worked for a couple of bakeries in the neighborhood," and he said "Me too. You really had to hustle, though, because you couldn't use the-bus-didn't-come excuse too many times." "But I'm curious. What reason Dad give you for telling all these stories?" and he said "He thought I might want to write about them. To quote him, or close to it, 'As long as you insist on sticking with this *meshugener* work that will only leave you lost and flat broke, maybe these will be interesting old-time Lower East Side stories you can use and possibly sell.'" "Will you use them?" and he said "So far it doesn't seem there'll be anything I can do with them, but you never know; one might start something when I least think about it," "And there was nothing, you say, about Sis and me in the letter?" and he said "Only what I told you: he was going to write you both." "So he wrote yours first. That makes sense. He wanted to get all the stories out before he forgot them. It's possible he then got too sick or weak or tired after. I mean, he wrote quite a letter to you, judging by the size of it and what you say, and thought he'd get to ours but something like what I said prevented him. Anything else he tell you I might not have heard?" and he said "I don't know. Shoveling snow for dough after the biggest blizzard to hit New York in twenty years?" "That one I know but I forget most of. Go on." "Nothing much. It paralyzed the city for weeks. He said he earned more in two weeks' shoveling than his father did at his job in a month, and he gave it all to them." "Grandpa was a darner and weaver and did most of his work at home, if I remember Dad correctly, which you'd think would bring in at least as much as shoveling snow. Maybe Dad worked two to three times as many hours as Grandpa averaged in a week, or it had something to do with Grandpa's drinking problem," and he said "He mentioned that too, somewhere else in the letter, but I forget in relation to what. Also, working in a cap factory for slave wages on Varick Street while in high school and nearly losing his hand in a textile cutting machine," and his brother said "We've both seen the scars. And don't you remember, he even once pointed out the building and floor the factory was in when we were all down there?" and he said "No, you must have been with him yourself or with someone else. But this I found interesting. His two months in the army during World War I. And being disappointed when the war ended and he was discharged because he'd just been, though the only horse he had ever been on before was attached to an ice wagon when he was a kid, accepted into the cavalry corps," and his brother said "Dad on a horse. I heard that one too." "So you know them all. He also went on about his sickness a little. Nothing disturbing. Just how he hated being not only enervated but also immobile, ineffectual, and unproductive, were the words he used, though there was nothing he could do about it. 'No reason for me to cry about my condition,' he said, 'since this is what life hands out if you live long enough, and if you don't believe that, you're a fool.'" "That's Dad all over. Part stoic, part lots of things, but never complaining about his illness that I ever heard. Of course, as Mom and I told him for years to do, if he'd gone to a doctor for a simple physical once before he reached sixty-five, maybe he would have lived a few years longer and avoided some of the complications he went though. But... so I guess that's it?" and he said "With this?" waving the letter. "Oh, some other stuff, but about me," and his brother said "Like what?" "My women. He thought they were all homely, lifeless, and takers. And that he continued to be disappointed that I'd gone into what I did for a living, quote unquote he wrote, but mostly repeats of what he'd told me countless times before. But one funny thing. Or not so funny. Anyway... that it never seemed to him that I'd shown any talent or the necessary skills for writing or what he saw as a deep interest in it, other than for reading, and which he thought one would have to have to become a writer. But that he wished me all the luck with it, not that he thought, hard as I was going at it and even now with all the stories he gave me, it would ever bring me anything but frustration, poverty, and worse. But, he added, people in more difficult fields, like acting, have beaten the odds and become stars when nobody thought they could, so why not me?" "Well, that, for Dad, was encouragement, and unusual. Makes me want to read the letter," and he said "I'd rather you didn't. Not because it's so personal. Other than for a couple of parts, it really isn't. Just that it was addressed to me and for some reason I want to keep it that way. I don't quite know what I meant by that. I suppose I'm saying that anyone else reading it, even my wife—even my reading it to her, word for word—would sort of break the spiritual bond I feel in the letter. No, that's not right either. So what am I trying to say? That I feel—this is mostly it, or I think it is—that I've told you just about everything—more than I really wanted to, to tell you the truth—and the rest I want to keep to myself. Maybe after a while you can have it—a month or so, if I don't lose it by then—but for now, confusing as my reasons have been, do you mind?" "No, of course not," his brother said, "and I can understand. First of all, it's your choice. But secondly, I might feel the same if in my search through Mom's things I do come up with a letter to me from Dad and you asked to see it. But then, you would already have yours, so after I told you a few interesting things that were in it, why would you want to read mine?" "True. Unless there was something about me you particularly wanted me to see."

DAUGHTER

THIS IS ALL in his head. His older daughter heads out of the house. He says "Hey, where're you going?" and she says "Out," and he says "But where, and with whom?" and she says "Friends. They're picking me up now." "Whose car is it?" and she gives the name and he says "Don't stay out too late, okay?" but the door's closing by then.

It's late and he says to his wife—this is all in his head— "She should be home by now. Or at least have called why she isn't home and where she is and when she's planning on getting home." "Don't worry, she's been out late before without calling," and he says "Never this late." "Why, what time is it? I don't have my watch on me"—saying this from her study next to the kitchen—and he looks at the clock on the stove and gives the time and she says "It is late, even for a Friday night. Who'd she say she was with?" "Friends, with Amy driving." "Do you have Amy's phone number, just in case?" and he says "Somewhere," can't find it, he'd written it on a take-out menu on the refrigerator door a while ago but the menu's not there. "Where's the Indian Café take-out menu that was on the refrigerator?" and his wife says "I didn't see

127

it, and when was the last time we had Indian food—a month ago, two? And you're the one who always does the ordering." "I'll check the phone book. What's Amy's last name again?—I always forget it," and she gives it and he gets the phone book from under her desk. "What the hell am I looking for? There are a million Moores here. You know her father's first name?" and she says no and he says "Maybe it'll come to me when I go down them. I know he told me it a couple of times when he brought Amy here before she got a car," and he starts from the top, sees a street name he thinks is Amy's from when he got directions to pick up his daughter at her house a few months ago and another time when he drove her there and says "Marvin and Jenna Moore? Sounds right, on Billings?" and she says "I wouldn't know. If I heard their names, I forget them, and you do all the driving, so I wouldn't know their address." "Something tells me that's it; 'Billings' more than their first names, though 'Marvin' now is also beginning to sound right. May I?" and unclips her portable phone from the front of her dress. "It's not too late to call?" she says. "Even for a Friday night, it's almost twelve and they may be sleeping," and he says "What else can we do? I'll explain; they'll understand," and dials, a sleepy man's voice says "Yeah?" He apologizes and explains, the man says "It's okay; done it myself a couple of times with Amy and her older brother. These kids are something, huh? Thank God it turns out always to be nothing. I think I heard Amy come in a short while ago, and alone. If she's already asleep, this is important enough to wake her. Hold on," and he comes back and says—this is all in his head—says what?

And what's he getting at with this? Something about his fears. Amy didn't drive his daughter home. "She wanted to when she was leaving the club they were all at, but a boy there... I should really put Amy on. This is too important to you for me to pass this information on secondhand, and you'll want to ask her questions I didn't. I know I would. Amy?" he yells. "Now my wife says I'm waking everyone in the house up. I'll get her," and a minute later Amy comes to the phone and says they were all at the club, his daughter met a boy there and wanted to stay longer and the boy said he'd drive her home. "None of us knew him but he seemed like a nice boy. He doesn't go to our school, nor do any of his friends." "What's his name?" he asks. She doesn't know. "Jeremy it could have been—that's what one of our other friends said, or else she said he looks like a Jeremy. Yeah, that was it. I thought she should come with me, though. After all, I drove her there so I told her I thought it was my responsibility to drive her back. But she said she'd be all right, and I couldn't exactly force her to drive with me, so I left." And the boy's school, he asks—where's he go? But she doesn't know. "So what was she planning, to be driven home by this boy and all his friends? I mean, she never saw him before; it could be dangerous," and she says "There were girls with these boys too, and they all seemed nice. I don't think anything will go wrong. I even now remember he goes to a private school in the county, but I didn't hear which one. But I'm sure he had his own car. That's right, she told me. She's staying with him and his friends and then he'll drive her home in his car." "What's the name of the club and where is it?—they could still be there. Damn, why didn't I think to ask you that first thing," and she gives the name and street it's on and he says "Think it'll still be open? Even if it isn't," though she says it's open till 1, "I should call."

He calls the club. This is only in his head. Woman who answers says she wouldn't know how to page his daughter if she was there. "There's no way." "But you have a microphone or some kind of sound system; you'd have to if you're a club, not that I'd know what the heck goes on there. Is it for music? It must be. So just interrupt it for a few seconds, or whatever's going on now, and ask this name I'm going to give you to call home. Or that might be too embarrassing for her, so for her just to come to your office or wherever you are—" "I'm at the juice bar," the woman says. "Then to there. If I don't hear from her in ten minutes, I'll call you back." "Make it fifteen, just to be on the safe side."

Calls back in fifteen minutes. This is just in his head. In the meantime he called his daughter's other friends who were with her at the club and they also didn't know the boy's name or what school he went to. "No one came to the bar about your call," the woman says. "You announced it a few times? The place was quiet when you did it?" and she says "As quiet as a club this size can get. But the announcement was loud and clear and repeated twice and I'm certain everyone but the out-of-reach people heard it." "You mean if they were in the washroom, which she could have been, or someplace out of earshot like that?" and she says "That too. But if she was in a washroom or one of the small chat rooms then I'm sure when she got back to the main part of the club a friend would have told her of the announcement." "All her friends left more than an hour ago. If she's there it's with people she just met, which is why I wanted her to call home. I don't want her leaving the club with strangers." "We get a nice crowd here, sir. Most aren't raucous and just like to have some clean fun. We do a good job of screening who comes in and also keep a tight control over the place and ask anyone to leave who's causing trouble. A few rascals manage to escape our clutches but they're mostly trouble only to themselves. If your girl does come up to me in the next half hour before closing I'll give her your message and tell her how concerned you are about her." "Could you make the announcement once more? Maybe she *was* in one of those side rooms and nobody told her she'd been paged." "Really, I've done all I can do for you and now have to get back to my work," and he says "Listen, I don't want to go above you, but can I speak to your manager?" "I am the manager and also part owner of the club."

So what does he do now? This is all in his head. But why's it in his head? Because his daughter's out. His wife's working at her computer in her study right off the kitchen but he never spoke to her about their daughter being late, because she isn't late. She just left, or about an hour ago. He checks his watch. But what the hell's he checking his watch for? He didn't look at the time when his daughter left. It just feels like an hour but it could be an hour and fifteen minutes, maybe a little more. The doorbell rang, he was in the living room—he's still there, in the same chair he hadn't been out of since about a half hour before his daughter left—and his wife yelled from the study "Come in." The friend came in—he knows who she is: Amy, his daughter's best friend for the last four years. She walked past him—he was reading and looked up and they exchanged hellos—and a few minutes later she and his daughter must have gone through his wife's study, which connects on its other side to one of the two doors to his older daughter's bedroom, because the next thing he knew—they couldn't have walked past him without him seeing or hearing them; he can get lost in his reading but never that much—the kitchen door to the outside was slammed shut and a car in the driveway started up and drove off. But he gets worried about his daughter being out at night sometimes, is what he's saying; that's why all that stuff was in his head. He sees the worst that can happen. Imagines it. About his children, not himself. If he drops his younger daughter off at the mall alone—this was the same when his older daughter was that age, and day as well as night—he often fears something terrible will happen to her there. Same with his older daughter when she gets picked up by a car at the house at night or calls from a party or movie theater, for example, and says he doesn't have to pick her up, as she's getting a ride home. Fears the car will get into an accident. Or that another car—this particularly at night—with a man or some men in it will trick them into stopping by saying or gesturing something that one of their tires is very low or flat—he's warned her about this and once mentioned the ruse to Amy, but they're young so could still fall for it—and then that man or the men will get out of the car and pretend to help them and grab his daughter or both girls and throw her into their own car and drive away. Fears that when she gets sick—fears this for both daughters, of course—she'll get much worse and possibly die. It's all in his head. None of these things ever

132

happened. Oh, they've been sick lots of times but not the way he just described. They've had streps and high fevers and disabling flus and sometimes trouble breathing but they never came close to death. And other scares with them, like the possibility of a tumor behind his younger daughter's eyes and coffee-colored marks on his older daughter's back that her pediatrician thought might be neurofibromatosis, but both times after tests it turned out to be nothing. He used to have some of the same fears for his wife. When she was pregnant with his older daughter especially. He used to fear when she drove alone that something would happen—an accident, men in cars, running out of gas in a bad neighborhood—and he'd lose her and the baby. He usually thought this when she didn't come home within an hour of when she said she would and hadn't called. Used to fear for his mother too. Mostly when she was old and would get a cold or flu and be laid up for days and he'd fear it'd go to her chest and because of her age she'd have to be taken to a hospital where she'd die. She was taken to a hospital several times when she got very sick or when the doctor over the phone thought she'd had, by the symptoms she gave, a heart attack or stroke, though she died at home. He was there when she died. The exact moment or when it seemed it was, sitting by her bed when she made some gurgling sounds in her throat and shut her eyes and seemed to die. She died a natural death, one could say. Was quite old and things went in her and she got worse but recovered and then got much worse and died. Something like that. He was there too, twenty-five years before, when his father died. Or right outside his hospital room while an emergency medical team worked on him inside. To keep him alive or help him die, he never asked, but his father had been comatose for a while and when the door opened and one of the doctors came out and motioned she wanted to talk to him he knew his father had died. Now his older daughter's out for the evening, he supposes. Amy's a very good driver, his daughter's said. And he once was driving behind them in traffic—just turned out that way; he was coming home from work and they were going someplace—and she did drive well, signaling at the right time, going at a safe speed, not making any wrong driving moves, and his daughter later told him they never knew he was in a car behind them for about a mile. He wishes she had said something to him tonight about where she was going and how late she was planning to stay out, but maybe she did to his wife. He'll ask. Anyway, he's sure his worries about her are ridiculous, unfounded… something, just in his head, and that everything will be all right.

He gets up and goes into the kitchen for a vodka and grapefruit juice and his wife says from her study "Long as you're there, can you get me some frozen yogurt?" "Sure," he says, and opens the refrigerator—wrong door, he thinks; Jesus, what's happening to his mind?—and opens the freezer compartment and sees three different containers of frozen yogurt and says "Which kind? There's Neapolitan, chocolate fudge brownie, and something called cherry fandango," and she says "You choose for me," and he says "How about all three," and spoons a tablespoon of each into a bowl and gives it to her. She holds the spoon in one hand, bowl in her lap, and says "Give me a kiss before I dip into this?" and he does and she starts eating. He looks her over to make sure she's okay for now: feet elevated on a cushion with a rolled-up towel separating the ankles, laptop computer's too near the edge of the studio bed so he pushes it a few more inches in, portable phone's within reach of the wheelchair she's in and pillow behind her back seems straight. "You're set? Anything else? I can leave?" and she says "Yes, thank you," and he goes into the kitchen to fix his drink. "Do I hear ice clinking?" she says after he drops two ice cubes into a glass and he says "Yes, you do, but go back to your work because I know what you're going to say. I should've shut your door before I got the ice. Or just lied to you and said something like, as if I were talking out loud to myself, 'Oh, I need some ice for seltzer.'" "You don't think it's too close to bed-time for another drink?" and he says "It's a good two hours before mine and, oh, how could I forget? I know; because my mind's going… but Amy and our little dear. Did they say where they were off to when they left?" and she says "A club to listen to music, though first a quick stop at Café Zen." "I thought so. She say when she'd be home?" and she says "She said not to wait up and she has the key." "Okay, she's of age," and she says "Not to change the subject back to where it originally was, but you had at least two drinks before dinner and around three fairly full glasses of wine with dinner, not that I'm measuring. So don't you think you've had more than enough—I'm talking about your health here—and where it might also interfere with your sleep?" and he says "Come on, will you? It's a weekend night. And I'm not a drunkard, for Christsakes," and she says "I never said that. But I was also wondering if the

drinking wasn't because you were worried about something," and he says "What's to be worried about? One kid's
at a sleepover; we know the folks, so nothing can go wrong
there. Other's with her closest friend who's a good driver
and also shows plenty of common sense, as do all her friends
it seems. So I'm not worried there either. There's nothing
I'm worried about now. The kids are fine." "Nothing else
bothering you? Me? Your work?" and he says "You're the
same. You're all right, aren't you?" and she says "As good as
can be expected, I suppose," and he says "So? And my work's
going as well as can be expected too, I suppose. I mean,
what do I ask? Nothing. I'm fine." "Okay, then," she says,
"good," and holds out her empty bowl with the spoon in
it. He washes them, puts them in the dishrack, makes his
drink, sits in his chair in the living room, picks up the
book he was reading and reads a few pages of it and gets
tired and dozes off.

His older daughter comes home. He's dreaming this.
She says "Hi, Daddy." He wakes up in the dream, book falls
off his lap. "Did I wake the book up," he says, "or did the
book wake up me?" "Neither," she says. "You were up. So
was the book, but now it's down," and she picks it up and
puts it on his lap. "I'm going to sleep and you ought to too,"
and kisses his cheek and leaves the room. His wife wheels
herself into the living room in the dream. She says "It's late,
we should get to bed." "Everyone's telling me what to do
tonight," he says. "Okay, maybe I deserve it." They go to
bed. He doesn't do any of the preparations he normally does
for his wife and him before they get into bed. He just
wheels her into the room and suddenly they're under the

covers, but he's on the side she always sleeps on and she's on his. "Something's wrong," and she says "What?" and he says "Oh, I guess nothing." Their daughter says from behind their bedroom door "You didn't ask me about tonight. I had a great time." "How did that happen?" he says and she says "I don't know; it went smoothly from beginning to end. Good night," and he says good night. "I don't want to read before I go to sleep," he says to his wife and she says "Neither do I." "But you never read in bed at night," and she says "Sometimes I do and tonight I might have," and he says "I don't want to continue to seem contrary, so I'll just say to that 'That's true.'" He turns off his light and then hers. Then, still leaning over her, he starts kissing her and she kisses him back. He pulls off her long-sleeved shirt, the kind he always puts on her before he helps her into bed, and feels her breasts. "Good God, my mind again," he says. "I forgot to take off your bra." "Don't worry about it. If you take it off now you'll only have to put it back on me tomorrow, and time's too dear," and resumes kissing him.

He's up; his daughter's nudging him. "Daddy. Mommy told me I should wake you so you can help get her ready for bed." "Oh, you're home," he says. "That's wonderful." "Why? I usually come home, even on weekends, and if I don't I always call you." "I know. I wasn't worried. You have fun tonight?" and she says "It was okay." "You get the same dish you two almost always order at Café Zen?" and she says "Which one?" and he says "The dish; tofu with spinach," and she says "Yes, but we also had cold noodles and steamed veggie dumplings." "I want to reimburse you for what it cost. How much do I owe you, including tip?"

and she says "I put it on the credit card. Amy's share also, since she's been driving me around a lot lately and paying for all the gas. Was that all right?" and he says "Sounds good to me. Anytime. And the club... You liked the music?" and she says "We decided to skip it tonight and go tomorrow. We were both tired," and he says "So that's why you're home so early." "It's not that early. But Mommy. She said she called out for you for about an hour but you must have been asleep." "I am; I mean I was. I even had a nice dream. Don't worry, it was finished, so you didn't wake me out of it. I'm very tired also. It's been a tough week at work and everything else. I'll take care of Mommy now, though. Thanks," and he looks for his book, it's on the floor and he picks it up, lost his place but that's okay, and puts it on the side table next to the glass and stands up. She says "I'm going to sleep now. 'Night, Daddy." "Good night, sweetheart," and yells out "I'm here, I'm coming," and goes into his wife's study.

PARTY

THIS HAS ALWAYS stayed with him. Rather, it comes back from time to time. Takes place at a party. He was around seventeen. No, he was sixteen, probably no less, because at seventeen he was in college and by then had stopped seeing most of his high school friends. Friends when he was in high school, he means, since they all went to different private schools in the city—some went to the same one—and he went to a public high school in the Bronx where for most of his three and a half years there he had only two friends, neither knew the other and both he never saw except in school and occasionally on the subway after school when he and one of them were going downtown to their jobs. That first half year after grade school he went to what was called an elite public high school—one of about five in the city you had to take a test to get into—but found it too hard and left before he flunked out. He went to the Bronx school, which he wasn't entitled to go to since it was out of his school district, because the one academic high school in his Manhattan district was known as one of the worst in the city and for having lots of hoods and some with zip guns and there had even been a couple of shootings in it. The Bronx school was supposed to be a little better academically than the Manhattan one but also had lots of hoods, which he didn't know about till he got there, and no doubt some had zip guns but he never heard of a shooting in the school or even a student showing a gun. He got into this school by giving the address of an aunt and uncle in the district and getting them to sign papers that he lived with them. Another reason he chose that school over let's say another one out of his district and certainly one closer to home—the Bronx one took an hour to get to by subway—was because his brother had gone to it. But that was when it was a pretty good school, his brother said, with no hoods in it and any boy—it was an all-boys school when he and his brother went—in the five boroughs could apply to it. His father had also gone to it but when it was in Lower Manhattan. In other words, the same school named after the same New York governor but it closed down and reopened sometime later in a new building in the Bronx long after his father had graduated from it. He at least thinks it was a new building—it looked like something built in the Twenties or Thirties—but he's getting way off the track. The party. It was on Park Avenue or Fifth. Definitely Park, since the apartment building, he remembers, was on the west side of the avenue, and if that were Fifth the west side of it would be Central Park. He went with several of his private school friends who knew the girl giving the party or knew someone who knew her and could use that person's name. Anyway, it wasn't a hard party to crash, as they used to call it. They just walked into the building's lobby, gave the name of the girl to the doorman, and he said something like "Are you young men invited?" and one of them said "Yes, sir. I believe"—this is the line they always used and they designated which one would say it before they went into the building—"the invitation for all of us is in one of these pockets," and started feeling inside his jacket and coat and looking very disappointed he couldn't immediately produce the invitation until the doorman said—this seemed to always happen—"It's okay this time; go up," and gave the floor and which elevator to take and the elevator man took them up. On Park and Fifth in that neighborhood most of the elevators then, and maybe still today, were hand-operated, if that's the right term for it. The elevator opened onto the party. In other words, this was the only apartment on that floor and the elevator door, after the car's cage door was pulled back, opened onto a small public foyer and the apartment door right opposite the elevator was open and they could see from the car before they even got out of it the party going on. He doesn't know why he's making this so difficult if not incomprehensible to understand. Or why he even thinks the elevator business is important to put in. Why he didn't just say they got off the elevator and went into the party. But he thinks he knows why. To show something about the building and apartment of the girl who gave the party and the time it took place and what he and his friends were like then. He can't just jump to the heart of the piece without anything surrounding it, can he? For instance: "This happened when he was sixteen and living in New York. A guy he knew or knew of from his neighborhood peed on a girl at a Park Avenue party he was at." It was an enormous apartment in an elegant old building. He saw that about the apartment when he walked around it, something he liked to do at most parties he went to and still does at new residences he's invited to though not as much: to see the way other people live, how their rooms are furnished, what they have on the walls, what books are out or are in the bookcases and records in the record cabinets, and things like that, or if they even have books. It was a duplex, maybe even a triplex, with terraces you could stand out on and see Central Park, so the apartment must have been many floors up to see above the buildings on Fifth. It might even have been the penthouse and a floor or two below. The girl's family must be loaded, he probably thought and said something about later to his friends. High ceilings, lots of fancy wainscoting, pilasters, he thinks the word is, chandeliers and oriental rugs and in several of the rooms, marble floors, and paintings all over, even in the master bathroom he went into just to see what it was like, some early religious ones with frame lights above them, a few of the etchings in the softly lit wood-paneled library looking like they were by Rembrandt or Dürer—he went a lot to the Met and Frick on his own then, felt he knew something about art just from having looked at it so much and reading about it a little, even thought at the time he wanted to study art history in college and become a museum curator. There were more than a hundred people there, nearly all of them around his age to a few years older. Most of the men in ties and sports jackets or suits, the women in dresses and that sort of clothing. Young people dressed differently for parties then. They dressed up. Most of them seemed and spoke like East Siders who went to private schools. He and his friends lived on the West Side. They'd taken a cab over. Probably met in front of the Tip Toe Inn on 86th and Broadway, which is where they usually met on nights when they were going to a party together. Hailed a cab in front of Tip Toe, as they called it. A Checker, probably with jump seats, so three to four in the back seat, two to three sharing the jump seats. Five passengers was the maximum allowed in that kind of cab then and no one up front with the driver. So the driver probably complained when six or seven of them got in the cab, and they said, or one of them did—this was never designated—"Don't worry, we see a cop, two of us will dive to the floor, and we'll give a much larger tip." They got into the cab by piling through the two passenger doors at once before the cabby had time to lock them or say anything like "Hey, only five, it's the law." That's the way they usually did it. They knew no cab would stop for them if they all stood together. So one of them—usually the best dressed—would hail it from the street while the others were on the sidewalk in twos and threes and the moment the cab stopped they'd run to both sides of it and get in. Only a few times did a cabby insist that one or two of them get out or that they all leave. If they didn't—that dive-to-the-floor and larger-tip line and then "Come on, we're all in already, we're not going far, so just get moving"—he'd say he was going to look for a cop and one time a cabby held up a tire iron or wrench and said how would they like getting their heads bashed in? Did they end up giving the cabbies a larger tip those times? Probably not even a normal one. Most of his friends came from wealthy homes and got big weekly allowances—he and another boy were the only ones who had jobs in high school—but they often said they were short when it came their turn to chip in for the fare. Then later when they'd all go to a restaurant like Tip Toe for a snack, and that was the one they usually ended up in after discussing a number of other eating places, these same guys would order club or nova and cream cheese or sturgeon sandwiches and, if they had fake ID's, a German or Dutch beer, while he'd stick with his two old standbys: egg salad or liverwurst on toasted rye and no tomato slices, which he liked, because that was extra, and water or milk. If he'd say "Wait a second. Before, you said you were too broke to pay your share of the cab fare and I had to put more in. So how're you going to cough up for your food here?" these guys would say something like "I suddenly found a twenty in my inside coat pocket" or "I borrowed it from I won't say who, since he doesn't want anyone else mooching off him. But why you making a court case out of it? You need some dough for a more expensive sandwich and a beer, I got enough on me now to loan you at low interest." One of them probably did jump to the floor if they saw a police car, but only as a joke. The low interest line: a joke. And from the floor: "Hey, it's more comfy down here than where you guys are; lots of room." Oh, they could be so stupid and juvenile when they were all together, he thinks. Alone, meaning just two of them, or maybe three, they could have some good serious conversations about any number of things, even ethics and books. He also regrets the way they treated most cab drivers and, if they weren't allowed into a building where there was a party they wanted to crash, doormen, when they went as a group. They once tossed a big metal trash can filled with garbage into a lobby after they weren't permitted up. They once, when several of them distracted the doorman, grabbed his hat off his head and ran outside and kicked it back and forth before one of them threw it on top of a passing car. They once… terrible things, which they thought were great pranks. When there were only two or three of them and they were told by the doorman they couldn't get in, they left politely. But get to the point or at least where you left off. They cabbed over, took the elevator up in this swanky old building, is what they used to call it—but went over that. Heard the party going on before the elevator reached the floor, but sort of said that too. They got rid of their coats in a room with about a hundred other coats on chairs and two single beds and other furniture and the floor. Then he walked around alone, inspecting the apartment as he said but also keeping a sharp lookout, is one of the ways they used to say it, for pretty girls. When they left the elevator and still had their coats on, he now remembers, and no doubt all excited they were going to have a great time, a girl in a satiny dress and he seems to remember pearls came over to them at the door and said "You fellows are…?" and one of his friends said "We're from Bosley, seniors," and she said "Oh, on the West Side. We don't have any other Bosley boys here that I'm aware of. I'm your hostess," and gave her name and shook hands with each of them as they gave their names. "You can deposit your coats in the bedroom at the end of that hall. Since I don't recall inviting anyone from Bosley, and all my friends know better than to invite more than one person without first consulting me, I feel I have to tell you to please behave. Enjoy yourselves." What a doll, he told his friends. That figure, her face. And thought: so poised and rich, gorgeous and obviously smart, and that last crack showed she didn't take any shit. But why would she ever throw such a big party? Or that's something he could have thought then in that way. Also (for he fantasized about her for weeks and looked her number up in the phone book—she had her own listing—and thought of calling her and even had the first line: "I wanted to tell you how I felt about that horrible pig at your party" and the excuse, once he told her what high school he actually attended, why his friend had said he also went to Bosley: "He just wanted to simplify things"): that he could really go for her but felt she was so sophisticated and mature that she probably only went out with Ivy League guys at least a couple of years older than him. He could say he was around that age, but would have to admit he was still in high school, so didn't see how he could work that part out. He hooked up with his friends after taking his walk around the place and they ate (huge carved turkey, big sliced ham, both on enormous silver platters on a long dining room table decked out with lots of fancy side dishes and other good foods), drank (two bartenders serving drinks—God, what the whole thing must be costing her folks, he probably thought), circulated (some of his friends—he didn't; he usually had trouble initiating conversations with girls and then sustaining them long enough where they could talk as if they hadn't just met—probably even got phone numbers from girls and addresses of potentially great parties for the next few weeks). Then in the apartment's foyer when he was passing through with one of his friends he saw someone he knew from the West Side, or knew of. Albie Gold. Very rich guy, around nineteen, trim mustache, slicked black hair with a slight pompadour, always dapperly dressed, liked to race up and down Broadway in the Eighties in his new red convertible just to impress guys and girls hanging out there, had a reputation for picking fights with much taller guys and beating the crap out of them and going for the nose with his fists with the intention of breaking it and sometimes stomping the guy on the ground after he threw or punched him there. This is what he'd heard about him. Even if half of it was true, he thought then, someone to stay clear of because he could get so freaking crazy. Short, maybe five-seven but built like an ironworks chimney, as they used to say then: broad shoulders, bulging chest, bull neck, arms where you could see his big biceps through the jacket sleeves. He didn't like the way he looked either: most times with a mean scowl or contemptuous smile or just eyeing you as if sizing you up for a fight. I. was a strong kid too, worked out but just to look good (mostly pushups and situps at home), best built and tallest of his friends—they'd nicknamed him Ox but mainly to make their group seem tougher than it was, since he didn't like to fight and would usually try to talk two guys out of one and was also afraid if he got in one or suck-er-punched he'd get his nose broken or head split or front tooth knocked out. He was also about half a foot taller than Albie, so another reason to stay out of his way: though he was around two years younger than him he was still in height and build the type he'd heard Albie liked to start up with. So what was this goon, he'd call him, doing at such a refined party? Maybe his date brought him, he thought. Guys like that: lots of dough to spend, his own snappy car, good-looking in a dark creepy way, and much different and maybe even more exciting than most rich college guys his age, can be attractive to some girls, he supposes, and probably other things he doesn't understand about it. Anyway, his thoughts then, but now to the point. Albie was with a dream of a girl: tall, nice and slim, long legs, blond hair that was probably also long but wrapped around and pinned up in back in what a girlfriend of a friend of his said was a chignon, a very sweet face. Looked like a model: the little nose, fashionable clothes, almost no breasts, and something about the way she stood and smoked that seemed like a pose. Albie was smiling at her in a normal way when they were all in the foyer near the front door and then said something like "You know what?" and she smiled at him and said "What?" and still smiling as if he liked her he said "You're nothing but a stupid cunt. As stupid as any cunt could be. You'd have to be to drink so much when you know you can't hold it and to say such stupid things. Look at your puss. Go into one of the bathrooms here and wash it and do something about your ugly breath and don't come out till you've sobered up." She said something like "I'll go and do what I please, and why must you talk to me like a brute?" and looked like she was going to cry. "Like a what? You're disgusting," and he slapped the cigarettes out of her hand—someone immediately picked it up and put it out—and grabbed her hair—this in front of about two dozen people by now—and pulled down on it till she was on her knees, shouting for him to get off, he was hurting her. He held her

down by the hair and with his other hand unzipped his fly
and took out his penis and started pissing on her while she
screamed and tried to get out of the way of his piss and
yelled hysterically "Oh no, look what you're doing, you're a
slob, someone help me, call the cops, stop, stop," but he
kept pissing on her and I. just stood there watching and then
turned away and wished he was much stronger and tougher
than Albie and not afraid of getting his nose busted and so
forth and he could grab him by the head and throw him to
the floor and stick his face in the piss and keep mashing and
banging his face in it and say "There, how's that for a
taste?... Go on, take some more, lap it up, you freaking
pig," and then give him a good chop on the back of his neck
and say "There's more of that if you want... I'll cut your stupid head off if you like," and then take off his jacket and
cover the girl and say "Here, get up, go to the bathroom,
we'll try to get you a different dress or something," and
escort her to the bathroom or ask some girls to take her
while he kept his eye on Albie in case he tried to jump him
and if he did he'd really let him have it, knock him out cold
if he had to, and then see if he could find her another dress,
or maybe there was a way to wash and dry the soiled one
without ruining it... this place must have a washer and
drier, probably in a special laundry room behind some doors
in the kitchen. But he just looked away while she was saying things like "Someone, please, look what he's doing to
me, help," but nobody seemed to make a move to or even
say anything to Albie to stop. Then he heard Albie say
"Finished, you stupid cunt," and I. turned to them. Albie
was shaking the drops off his penis at her and then stuck it

back into his pants, zipped up, and got his coat from a foyer closet—he must have got to the party early to have put it there or just felt that's where his coat goes, not in the back like everybody else's—and left with another guy. The girl was still in the same position on the floor, sobbing, piss on her, around her. Then two girls bent down to talk to her, helped her up, and walked her out of the room. The hostess ran into the room right after, asked what happened and who made that mess? And he wanted to go over and tell her but a few people got to her first. "What an awful party, for something like this to happen," he said to his friend, and his friend said "I know, I never saw anything like it. Took out his shlong in front of everyone and didn't care how long they looked." "Awful, awful, awful," he said. "We should've jumped in, you and I, and maybe yelled for some other guys to, and got him away from her," and his friend said "He would have clobbered us both, and nobody else would have jumped in. He's a maniac; you saw. You can't fight a guy like that. He'd go crazy and wild and never stop coming at us and hitting and kicking till one of us was almost dead. The guy's strong as an ape. Someone once said they saw him lift the front of a car by himself. A small car, maybe a Nash, but all by himself and held it up for a minute—someone was counting—and then let it down slowly, didn't just drop it. And maybe she had a part of it coming. Not that way, peeing on her, but she might have done or said something he didn't like and he exploded. You go with a nut like that, you got to expect such things." "Ah, come on, there's no excuse for what he did. And he's probably a big liar too, because she didn't seem high to me." "Okay," his friend said, "it was terrible, you're right, but now it's over, she's being taken care of, so let's forget it; it's party time again," and he said "For me, it just makes me too sick to stay." "Don't be an idiot," and he said "No, I'm going," and his friend said he was staying, and he said "Tell the guys I left then," and he got his coat and left. It was around Christmas, he just now remembers. When school was out, and it was probably a Christmas party, which could explain all that kind of holiday food. And there was a decorated Christmas tree in the apartment, which is another thing they saw the moment they got out of the elevator, with a white sheet or layer of cotton underneath and lots of wrapped presents on top. And when Albie pulled the girl down by her hair she grabbed onto the tree for support and it came down with her and all the lights on it suddenly went out. Still, no one protested or stepped in.

THREE NOVELS

WHO WOULD'VE THOUGHT? This idiot writes a book and a publisher actually accepts it and then publishes it. Who would've thought it'd be reviewed and taken seriously and some are even great reviews in very good places? Who would've thought this inarticulate not very smart guy who has little to say to people in regular life and isn't very clever or funny or anything like that... is dull, in fact, and nobody has ever really paid much attention to him and certainly not to anything he previously wrote or at least not anywhere but the smallest places and who doesn't do well in social situations and even his own kids make fun of him sometimes and is one stinking college teacher, would write a book and everything like what he said would happen to it? It's amazing. He's amazed. He can't believe it. Really, he sometimes can't. He'd like to pinch himself. "Tell me it isn't true," he says. "Tell me and I'll believe it. Because of all guys for this to happen to?" But it is true. He has the book to prove it. With his name on the cover and the title he gave it and his face on the flyleaf, he thinks they call it, of the dust jacket. And the words in the book he wrote and all the ideas, everything, the images, dialog, characters... he created it all. And it's not a small book either. It's huge, in fact, and people are impressed by its size and weight and also that the long paragraphs fill up almost every page. But he isn't impressed by anything about it except that a schmuck like himself, and he doesn't think he's being too hard on himself by saying that, was able to sit down for years while doing all the other things he had to do at the time—teaching, marriage, kids, looking after his mother—and write a book, or manuscript, he should say, and send it out and that the first publisher to see it liked it enough to publish it and with very little editing work because they said it didn't need much and it did fairly well for a book by an unknown writer with no connections and was even nominated for a bigtime prize and... and... Just that he did it and wrote another huge dense one under the same circumstances— teaching, marriage, kids, looking after his mother till she died—and the publisher wants to publish this one too and maybe the same things will happen to it. Reviews, etc. Probably not the nomination and maybe the reviews won't be in such good places or as many, though who can tell? But amazement by everyone who knows him or who knew him back when that a guy who showed little to no promise for about forty years in anything but being almost a total fail- ure in life, if that can be called promise—in school, jobs, with women till he met the one who became his wife, and that such a bright wonderful woman went for him and con- sented to marry him when he asked is still something he finds hard to understand why—could write a book like that and that it got what it did and then write another one that might get the same things and maybe even more. But anyway, two fat and what some people even call complicated books in a row when probably nobody but his wife, and since he never asked her he can't even be sure of this, thought he had the ability and intelligence to write and publish anything but perhaps a brief letter on a mundane subject in a small newspaper that publishes every letter sent in other than obscene and inflammatory ones. He doesn't know how it happened but it did and he's not pleased by it all, just amazed—and using that word or its variations four to five times in so short a space shows how unimaginative and unresourceful a writer he is—that he was able to write those books, and he knows he's repeating himself again, and that all of what he spoke about before happened to them. Amazing. He's slapping, literally, his face to wake up.

"Hello, is this the writer who had his book reviewed in the *New York Times* today?" and he says "Yeah, what can I do for you?" "I just want to say that I read it, got your phone number from your publisher's publicist when I told her I was a movie producer interested in finding out from you if a movie option's been taken on it," and he says "It hasn't, as of yesterday. The person to speak to should be my agent, whose number I'll give you, though I'll gladly tell you anything you want to know about the book," and the man says "No, that movie-producer line was just my way of getting your phone number, since I'm sure they don't give it out to just anybody, and I'm only calling to say I thought the reviewer was absolutely right. Or let me put it differently:

was all wrong. Or maybe not *all* wrong, but a lot wrong."
"Thank you, I think, because I'm a little confused by that
'absolutely right' business becoming 'totally wrong,'" and
the man says "I said 'all wrong,' but I quickly corrected
that. I agree with some of the things the reviewer said, the
ones where she really socked it to your work, and also did a
number on you personally. But in some things she didn't go
far enough, which is why I settled on saying 'a lot wrong.'"
"Well, thanks again, that's very nice of you. A very cheerful
phone call to get a few minutes after my baby fell out of her
crib and split her head and we're now preparing to take her
to the hospital. And a half hour before that accident, a
phone call from my mother saying my father died in his sleep
overnight and would I come to New York immediately to
help her." "You're kidding me now. And I have to tell you
that your humor, which is one of the things I really find
unsavory and juvenile in your work, is, well, unsavory, juvenile, and tasteless. One shouldn't kid like that about one's
children or any children in the way you did, making fun of
serious accidents and illness and potential tragedy and possibly even death. As for your father—" and he says "But it's
true, and that wasn't all. Early this morning—maybe ten
minutes after I woke up, so we're saying three hours ago,
since I slept late for me, though she said she couldn't sleep
a wink all night over what she was about to tell me—my
wife told me—" and the man says "Ah, you're full of it,"
and he says "Maybe I am, maybe I'm not. Okay, I'll be honest: I am full of it about my father; he died more than fifteen
years ago. But I'm not full of it about my baby daughter.
And since my wife almost has her dressed now and says we

156

should get ready to go—and of course everything she told me this morning has to be put off till our baby gets taken care of—I'll have to—" and the man says "I happened to know both your daughters are past being babies. That's what it says on your book cover. It doesn't say that specifically, but just that on the jackets of your two books I read it talks about you having two daughters, so they couldn't be babies considering how many years ago the earlier book came out, " and he says "Excuse me a second," and says away from the phone "Okay, okay, I'm coming. Just one minute; let me take care of this," and says into the phone "You must've heard; my wife wants me to hang up. The bleeding's stopped, the baby seems okay, but we still want to check her out at the hospital. Before I go, though, I want to know one thing. Why'd you call? I mean, granted you didn't know how bad things were for me here at home. But who calls up to tell a writer who's just received an extremely mean review of his newest book, which he spent more than three years working on, though of course you couldn't have known that too—but in the most influential newspaper in the country for books, that the book was even worse than the reviewer said? Is this your idea of a joke? Do I know you? Are you the same comedian who called me at 6 a.m. one day last year to say I'd won a MacArthur Genius Grant? Did I once give you a B in my rudimentary fiction-writing course when you thought you deserved a B+?" "I'll tell you what kind: someone who detests your work, thinks it's less than mediocre and is infuriated that inferior writers like yourself get published while his own work, which is ten times as good as yours—twenty, thirty; infinitely better, I'm saying, and in

every way: story, style, language, rhythm, and so forth—
gets turned down by editors and agents alike over and over
again." "Oh, now I understand; all right, good. But just
know that if you call again I'm hanging up," and he hangs
up. The phone rings a minute later and he answers it and
says "I know, it's you, saying you want to hear me hang up,"
and the man says "No, as you well know, I heard you hang
up the last time. I'm calling to say that everything I told
you in my last call was the truth. That you shouldn't think
I was saying it out of jealousy or revenge. I do feel that way
about your work. It stinks, it's dreadful, it smells to high
heaven, a whiff of it can knock a strong man out. You are
without doubt the world's worst published writer I know of,
I only read your work to get an occasional rise as to how bad
it can be, and that this phone call isn't a joke, and now you
can hang up," and he says "I have to, because suddenly my
little baby's taken a turn for the worse. I also want you to
know, just to get all the facts straight so that you don't
think I was lying about her before, and I'm saying this as
I get my coat on and look for my gloves, that she was born
after the cover for my new book went to print. We knew she
was going to be a girl and that she'd be several months old
by the time the book came out, but thought it'd be bad luck
to mention a third child in the jacket copy before she was
born," and hangs up.

He gets an envelope in the mail. No name or return
address on it. It's thick and letter-size and before he opens it
he thinks "I bet someone's sent me a short story to read."
One of his former students: they do that from time to time,
without asking him. Or someone who doesn't know him

but thinks he might like it enough to want to help get it published. That's happened a few times too. Or it could be an offprint of a published story or literary article from a friend or former student: that would be okay if it isn't too long. The unpublished stuff, which he's expected to give critical comments or advice on, he hates getting: takes up too much time, and he's already got enough manuscripts to read from his teaching. At the top of the first page—no title below, so it probably isn't a story, or name or return address on the page either—is written in pencil "This turned out to be much longer than I anticipated or wanted, but I hope you'll read every word of it at least twice so it'll wholly sink into your skull." Kind of harsh, that skull, and sinking into it is almost menacing, so he now thinks it's from someone who doesn't much like him or his work: a long diatribe or cranky criticism, even. He's also gotten a couple of those over the years from people he didn't know. The rest of what's on the page was typed on a computer and printed out. Right under the penciled message is the date: same day the envelope stamps were canceled in Philadelphia two days ago. Knows or has known a number of people from there and the surrounding area. He reads the first sentence: "I've thought of writing you this for the last ten years, or ever since I read that long section about me in your third novel, I believe it was." So it's a letter. And third novel? The big one, if this person's got it right. There were several long sections in it about certain people who played an important part in the narrator's life—one, a single paragraph that went on for a hundred pages, but that was about his father. Which section could this person have been in, if she, since the only other long section about a male was the one of his brother, isn't imagining it? He goes to the last page and it's unsigned. What's going on here and what's she going to say? He's done with his work today, has nothing to do the next half hour till he leaves to pick up his younger daughter at high school, and sits down at the dining room table to read it. No salutation either, he just notices. He should get himself a mug of coffee or tea as a pick-me-up. Nah, stop stalling, just read; the coffee or tea he'll have when he gets back home. If it's truly bad, really insulting, well, it's just a letter. "I've thought of writing you this" and so on. "I actually wrote you several letters, maybe a dozen over the years, telling how I felt about that section and especially the part concerning my sister's death. I tore them all up because I decided each time that I'd only written it to get my revulsion for you out of my system and that I didn't want to have even a one-sided communication with you or receive an apologetic or explanative letter in return, kneejerk or sincere, if that's what would have been your response. One letter was even in my mailbox, some fifty feet from the house I lived in then, sealed and stamped, of course, and waiting to be picked up by the mailman. He always drove up at the same time, between 2:00 and 2:15, and I'd stuck it in a half hour before that, thinking yes, finally you should learn how your book affected my life since I read it, and for a month, I'd say, devastated me with your exploitation of my deepest grief. Does that sound overdramatic? What of it, for it's the truth. But when I saw—I was watching for it from my kitchen window—the truck drive up and the mailman stick his arm out of it to open the mailbox and take the letter and put some mail in and flip the mailbox flag, I again thought No, it's not worth it, for the same reasons I had before, and ran out of the house and down the driveway yelling for him to stop, since he'd already started off, and got the letter back and right in front of him ripped it up. I even recall what he said when I did it: 'Geez, that had to be one letter you didn't want the addressee to read.' Why is today's letter different in that I intend to send it? (Otherwise, it's pretty much the same letter I've been writing you approximately one a year of for ten years, other than for this explanation as to why they were never sent.) The truth is, I still don't know if I will send it or if it'll even get as far as the mailbox, which in this house is only a short walk from the front door, easier to get to than the previous one and a lot faster to retrieve anything you put in but at the last moment didn't want sent. The principal reason, if I send it, and I'm almost sure I will, but judging from my track record with these letters I shouldn't be so confident, although I never before thought I would mail it as much as I do now (with the one that got into the mailbox, I really, while sitting in the kitchen watching out for the mail truck, knew I'd grab it back before the truck arrived or took it away) is that I now think my writing these letters and then destroying them has in no way diminished my anger to you in what you did. But if I do mail it—it makes no difference to me if you receive it, since if I don't get a response I'll assume you decided to stay silent or abided by my wishes not to answer me—I think I can completely close this odious episode with you for the rest of my life. Though we'll see how I feel about that after I mail it, if I do. But some questions, which are in all my previous letters to you, plus or minus a few. Why did you have to write about Elise's suicide when you wrote that long section about me? Why did you even have to name her Eliza, which is as close as one can get to her real name? 'Susan' wouldn't do? 'Jane,' 'Jill,' 'Penelope,' 'Pam'? Did you have to describe in vivid detail the trauma the surviving sister went though? Equally disturbing: did you have to make them sisters? Elisa couldn't have been a man? Would it have been less painful to Gwen, which is also as close to my name as one can get, if it had been her brother who killed himself? But if you had to make them sisters, you couldn't have said Eliza was older than Gwen by a year or that they were twins? Have you no imagination? Aren't novelists supposed to have elaborate imaginations, able to change facts and details around believably and make any incident go a dozen different ways? Shouldn't there be some unwritten code fiction writers have regarding concealing the identities of the real people they're writing about? Is there a reason why you had to stick so close to what happened in everything in the section about me? How you found out—the snooping that must have been done to get it down so accurately—I don't even want to go into. But tell me: simply by changing around the letters of our names a little and nothing else, made you think you were writing a work of fiction and not a memoir or journalism? For example: did you have to include the television documentary about war my family and I were watching when your Eliza and our Elise excused herself from the living room and a minute or so later squeezed herself out of my parents' bathroom window? What would it have taken to have said it was a regular weekly TV show, even given the name of the series, and if you didn't think we as a family would watch one, then said we were all sitting around the dining room table having dinner or lunch? Did you also need to say that your Gwen was the one who first felt a breeze coming through the apartment, or the first to speak about it, told her parents a window must be open, volunteered to get up and shut it and found the bathroom window wide open and immediately sensed what had happened because of Eliza's terrible depression the last few months and crept up to the window and took a minute before sticking her head out and saw Eliza's body in the courtyard ten stories below? Did you get all that information from someone I know, because the part about creeping and waiting and looking wasn't in the newspapers, since my parents and I refused to be inter- viewed? And what would it have taken to say Eliza landed on the street? Wouldn't that have been even more sensa- tional, though all right, maybe that's what you wanted to avoid? But would it have mattered much if you had said Eliza took poison, sleeping pills, asphyxiated herself with gas in our kitchen when she was alone, slit her wrists in the bathroom she jumped out of, or while waiting on a subway platform with Gwen, if you felt you had to have Gwen there when she died, threw herself under a train? Did you also have to give the exact location of our building? You did— tactfully, you must have thought—hold back from giving the building's number; but 'southeast corner of 86th Street and Riverside Drive' and same apartment number we had? Would this section have been any less if you had said '11E' instead of '10B,' or even '10A' or 'C,' and put us on West

End Avenue in the 70s or 90s? Is there a literary purpose behind this that I'm unaware of? Did you expect readers to adore your novel so much that they'd want to make pilgrimages, à la Joyce and Eccles Street, to 86th and Riverside and point to the building and say 'That's where Eliza's suicide took place—you can't see where she landed because it's in a rear courtyard, though maybe the super will let us have a peek—and where Gwen first started cracking up over it?' You had to say Gwen's father was a pediatrician and her mother an economics professor? You couldn't have even switched those two professions around? A woman pediatrician married to an economics professor just didn't seem believable to you? You had to say Eliza had a chipped front tooth and saintly smile as a kid and a beauty mark over her left eye? You couldn't have said she had perfect teeth and a crooked smile and the beauty mark was over her right eye? You had to use the real name and nationality of our cook? You had to give the unusual breed and sobriquet of our dog? You had to describe our living room right down to the green-striped slipcovers and the silver Ronson cigarette lighter on the glass coffee table? The Dürer woodcut and Modigliani drawing and Braque collage in the dining room? Raphael, Miró, Sigueiros, Soutine? None of them were familiar to you? You never heard of any other artist but the ones we had? Or any other medium they worked in but the ones we owned of theirs? What is it with you, or was? But that should be enough. Because you get my point. You went too far and you didn't invent and you had no sensitivity to my feelings. You should have thought, since you portrayed me in the section as a very well-read literary young woman, that if I saw or heard about a book of yours I might go out of my way to read it. And that if it were billed, as it was on the book jacket and mentioned as such in the one review of it I read, as deeply autobiographical, I might be additionally interested in it to see what this often moody and opinionated but high-minded do-gooding high school boy I knew had done with his life and what kind of person—here I'm referring to quality—he turned out to be. You also should have thought that if you brought up my sister's suicide in the guise of Eliza in such detail and the effect the narrator heard it had on me and my family—that I had a breakdown over it, as you wrote about Gwen, and my up-till-then vigorous, healthy father died weeks after Elise's death of a heart attack on the street, and my mother was never the same after it either—that it would be extremely painful to me. I'm sure you knew something like that would happen—a dumb person with few insights into human nature doesn't write it on the grounds that art supersedes the feelings of the real people the so-called artist is writing about. Is that it? I bet it is, or very close. For you had to know that my reading it would relive the events for me—feeling the breeze, looking out the window, seeing her body, knowing instantly my dear sister was dead—in the most… well, I already said 'painful,' so in that way. But I think you made a big mistake. The section would have been much better—you know, I don't like pointing out the weaknesses of a writer's work once it's in book form (if it was in a magazine it could always be changed later for the book), but I've no regrets telling you—if you had concentrated solely on a young man experiencing unrequited adult romantic love for the first time. That would have meant leaving out my sister except perhaps as a walk-on for color: she opens the front door for his first date with Gwen, smiles her saintly smile and snaps her gum and then goes to her sister's room to tell her, or undignifiedly yells from the foyer, as you had it (I'll take your word that's how it went, since you seemed to get the rest right: Elise did at that age love to snap gum) that her date's arrived. Keeping, in other words, the section to just Gwen and your narrator: the first (and perhaps the seminal one) of a string of hopeless and tormented relationships he had with women till he's around forty-five would have been artistically stronger and narratively more consistent with the rest of the novel, which recounts, after several comical smittenness and sex incidents with girls when he was grow-ing up, a haphazard chain of love entanglements, one worse and longer than the next, till he finally clicks with a woman who, soon after they marry and quickly have two kids, gets sick and he had to start taking care of her more and more as the novel ends. (That this happened to you, and again I assume it did, since nothing of which I know about me and my family in that section seemed made up, I take no pleasure in, though I feel a heck of a lot sorrier for the woman—your wife, who I hope by now has fully recovered or certainly not got worse.) Anyway, the section should have been limited to just Gwen and him, rather than throwing in everything you knew about my family including the his and her sinks and hair dryers in my parents' bathroom (why did you ever think you were allowed in there? I had to have told you it was forbidden and that even we kids had to stay out and use our own bathroom or the guest one), none of which applied to his life. It also, of course, would have spared me the grief you gave. Just the following would have been all you needed: he meets Gwen at her school dance, pretends to be a preppie from Connecticut so he can get past the mothers at the entrance table barring public school students from crashing the dance, he eyes her and she eyes him (you looked better from across the room than up close, by the way), he introduces himself clumsily, they talk, find they have similar interests (books, classical music, art museums, legitimate stage), date awhile (she sort of knew from the start that as a couple they'd never amount to anything but would go out with him till someone more attractive and older and with a bit more personality and the keys to his family's car came along), kiss goodnight at her door a couple of times, even neck in the balcony of a movie theater for a few minutes, but only because she felt she needed practice at fifteen and he, a year older and because of their goodnight kissing, gave the impression he was experienced at it, and then when she sees he's beginning to like her a lot more than she could ever like him (calls almost every night, wants to date her once every weekend) she says she thinks they should cut down on the number of times they see each other (every other week or so and usually on a weekday night so she can keep the weekends free for parties or another fellow who might call), he gets into a snit, rails at her that it must be some other guy she's now seeing: 'A rich prick from a snobby private school, someone on his way next year to Harvard or Princeton or Yale or maybe he's already there and invites you up for boola-boola weekends and takes you to expensive places because his parents give him a fat allowance,' and things like that, scaring her with his anger—she never had a boy yell at her like that before—but scares her so much that she's now convinced she shouldn't ever see him again, and later he tells himself, as you wrote, and I'm sure this is true too—why should you all of a sudden start making things up?—that he doesn't think he can live without her, which is absurd or just sad for a boy his age to believe, especially when she never once said she had any real affection for him—the kissing didn't count; all her friends did that after the second or third date; after all, it was a progressive school they went to, but she bets parochial and public high school girls did it too and possibly went farther and also with boys they didn't especially care for— or that he was the only one she wanted to go out with, though I suppose his feeling so low over it could happen, but it did indicate to her at the time that he was a little disturbed and absolutely the wrong fellow for her. So. So, he gets over it in a few months, you wrote, or almost does, but is noticeably depressed during much of this period, his brother trying to console him by saying it happens to everyone, boys and girls both, so it'll happen to her too and then she'll know what he went through, and his father telling him—I can honestly say that this part was the one I liked most in the section; it went beyond just lifting from life and was funny and the father came out as the most vivid character in the book, or the half I read of it (for the book did go on and was overlong for what it ultimately delivered) in your quick picture of him—that no woman, not even a beautiful young rich one (your words, not mine, and though I was at your apartment once for a party your brother gave,

which wasn't in the section—you must have forgot it—
I don't ever remember meeting your parents) whose grand-
father, a successful dress manufacturer, as was mine, could
one day bring him into the business if he stuck with her, is
worth getting so dejected over; 'Your kid gets chronically
ill; one of your parents die? Then I can see it.' During those
months of depression he continues to call her and she starts
hanging up every time she hears his voice on the phone.
Eventually she asks her parents and sister and anybody else
who answers the phone there to ask who it is if it's a boy
calling her so that she can avoid talking to him, though he
manages to get around that a couple of times by disguising
his voice and telling Eliza, I think it was, that it's Chip or
Chuck or Preston or George. They never see each other
again after that, though he claims to have spotted her from
a bus window when she was around twenty-four, walking
across Broadway in a summer dress and sun hat and suntan
and sandals and looking more beautiful than he's ever seen
her, he says. That's where the section should have stopped:
with that short coda, though even that didn't seem necessary. Because why was he so sure it was her? Her appearance
might have changed much more than he realized in eight or
nine years—I did grow another two inches and of course
filled out a little and even my hair color wasn't the same—
and the woman he saw could have been someone he only
imagined she'd look like at twenty-four, with the same
height, weight, face, build, and hairstyle that Gwen had at
fifteen. But you continue the section to its detriment. When
he tries phoning her the same day he saw her from the bus,
thinking if she was unattached or even if she wasn't she

might after all these years consent to have a coffee or lunch
with him just to catch up on their lives, though I think that
would be more of a reason for him than her, he finds she and
her family aren't in the phone book and Information tells
him that no one with her name or her father's or sister's has
a listed or unlisted number in the entire city. If you had to
go on after the breakup, I would have left it at that: a simple
conclusion, end of encounter, on to the next section and
episode of his life, rather than have him call up the only person he knows of who knew Gwen after high school—this
seemed, even if it was real, a bit too convenient, and I've no
idea who it was: a fellow you say was in her freshman class
at college ('She was the campus beauty the short time she
was there,' the man had told him a while ago, although
I hardly think I was; 'every guy wanted to go out with her
and get into her pants if he could and she was a sure bet to
be homecoming queen her sophomore year if she hadn't
transferred,' and you can see why I did: what jerks!)—and
learned that 'Eliza' had killed herself the year before and
that the family, he heard, wanting to get out of the apartment and city she did it in, moved somewhere out of town.
Over the years, I suspect, you learned more about the suicide—the details—and what had happened to me and my
parents, all of which you found necessary to stick into this
stupid section about me. But there was no reason to. The
tragedy of my sister and then my going crazy for a while and
having to be hospitalized and the sudden death of my father
and also the chronic depression of my mother after Elise's
death till she too died of (and melodramatic as this word is
I can't think of a more suitable one for it) heartbreak, didn't

illuminate anything about Gwen and himself. The section should have been over by then. I know I've said that. Or, which I've also said, you could have ended it with him thinking he sees her from the bus and being unable to locate her in the phone book, but that's all. The sister and parents just as side characters, as with your father and brother, would have been enough and in fact was necessary, I now see, since without them we might have thought Gwen and he were orphaned single children living alone. But the suicide? (And God knows why I thought I had to make a joke with that last remark, for I find none of this funny.) If you had been more professional and perceptive and accomplished as a writer in this section you would have known it dominates every action around it and eclipses every scene that comes before it. In any event, I think I've gone on more than enough and said everything I wanted to say. And the letter's definitely going out. I'll get your address somehow without having to send it care of your present publisher or school. Before, I used to address the letters I was thinking of sending you to your mother's when she was still in the phone book and living in the same building you grew up in. This time, just to be sure you'll get it, because I don't want this to have been one big waste of time, I'll get your address from the phone book of the city the jacket of your most recent book says you live in, and if you're not listed or there anymore, then from your school directory. And, if I haven't said so yet, and I'm not about to read over what I wrote so far to check whether I have—if I'm repeating myself here and have done so elsewhere, and maybe even repeats of repeats, what of it? This isn't serious literature I'm trying to write but a very angry letter with elements in it that have tormented me for years—I have to let you know how much I still hate you for what you wrote about Elise (not the kid-sister part but the suicide) and for not trying to disguise it if you had to write it (that I know I've said, as with the line about 'torment' above) and also for your insensitivity to my feelings (that too), which seems, now that I think of it (so something new), odd coming from someone who had been an easily hurt oversensitive young man, though they probably go together: you finally got even with me for causing you such misery (and don't think I didn't know and sympathize with you a little then, but what was I supposed to do, continue to go out with you when I no longer wanted to and even started getting a little afraid of you? Damnit, I was fifteen!) and also felt that by writing about it you were able to make the most of your miserable situation, because isn't that what writers too often do with their and other people's experiences: exploit what hurts? Anyway, a good place to end the letter, I'd think, but something tells me it's not. If this is to be the one letter I send you (there can't be any more, for in this one I feel I've said it all) then it hasn't brought me the emotional relief I'd hoped it would. A letter's just too damn impersonal for what I want from one in this. I'm missing out seeing your reaction when you read it, which might be very little, since, after so many years, the incident's long past to you, the book's old stuff, you've gone on to new things, etc., so why would you care, or care a lot, and you might even think I'm making more out of it than I should or making up most of what I feel. Maybe the only thing that would give me relief... yes, I really think this would do the trick—" Just then his wife comes into the room, and he quickly tries to finish the sentence: "so I might, I just might, because—" and says "Is that mail?" and he says "All there is of it other than for a few circulars and a request from some charitable organization, but addressed to me this time, so I took the liberty of throwing it out," and she says "What's that you got, a letter?" and he says "A very long one," and she says "Who from?" and he says "Someone from way back who just caught up with me," and she says "He or she read one of your books and wrote you about it?" and he says "Something like that. A girl—a girl then—I knew from my old West Side teenage days," and she says "Anything interesting?" and he says "Not really. Repetitive, which because of its length—look how many pages," and he holds them up, "I think it'd almost have to be, and hard to read also: single-spaced and minimal margins... I'll tell you about it later," and she says "Aren't you going to be late picking up the kid?" and he says "I was just going," and folds up the letter and puts it back in the envelope, thinks he'll finish it in the car while waiting for his daughter to come out of school, and gets up and sticks it in his back pocket and then thinks No, I've read enough of it and I'm not going to try to answer her, and in the kitchen drops it in the bag for recyclable paper as he leaves the house.

WIFE

HE WOKE UP, looked at the clock on the windowsill. It was almost five, so time to turn his wife over on her back. He went around to her side of the bed, pulled the covers aside, took the pillow out from between her legs and the rolled-up towel from behind her back, and with his right arm lifted under the knees where in one motion he got her on her back. He straightened out her legs, stuck a small couch pillow between her feet so they wouldn't rub against each other and cause an abrasion that could lead to a bed sore, put a bed pillow between her knees and covered her and got back in bed. He faced her and put his hand on her left breast. He liked better holding her breast while she was on her side with her back to him. Her breast felt larger that way, there was more to hold, while when she was on her back it felt kind of flat. When they first went to bed or after he'd put his book down and turned off his bedlamp and she was already asleep, he always put his hand on her breast, sometimes cupped it, sometimes just covered it, often in both cases with the nipple in the crook of his index and middle fingers. He liked holding her this way and it helped get him to sleep.

But after about thirty seconds she pushed his hand away and said "Don't touch me. It keeps me awake." He kept his eyes shut. Maybe she was looking at him. Daylight came early in July in Maine and there was already enough of it for her to see him. He wouldn't say anything, wouldn't look at her. She'd never pushed his hand away like that before. She always seemed to like his hand there, or never complained of it. Oh sure, "Don't touch me!" after they'd had a serious argument and he was trying to make up in bed. But this was different. No argument. He'd got her set for sleep on her side, read a little, and then gone to sleep snuggled up to her with his hand on her breast. He even stroked it a little, stroked her buttock and leg too, and then put his hand back on her breast and fell asleep. If he turned on his side with his back to her, which he wanted to do, since lying this way without holding her was getting physically uncomfortable, she might take it as a sign he was angry. He didn't want her to think that. It would make him seem childish. He wanted her to think he was already asleep and what she'd said and done had meant nothing to him. That if she didn't want his hand there, it was all right with him. That he could understand why she might not want it. For the reason she gave. That it kept her awake. Or at least understand it for tonight. But did it mean the beginning of something new in her sleeping habits? That from now on, even when they first went to sleep, she won't want his hand on her breast? He'd hate that. He'd say "But you know that holding your breast, or both at the same time sometimes, helps me fall asleep." Suppose she then said "Then find another way of getting to sleep, because your holding me like that wakes me and then keeps me up. It has most times before but I never said anything because I knew how important it was to you. But I can't let you do it anymore, except maybe for a short time after we make love." She could say that and more. Was she looking at him? His eyes were still shut. Pretend to sleep. Maybe she'd forget what she said tonight. Maybe even if he brought it up she wouldn't remember. Or maybe she'd say, without him even bringing it up, that she changed her mind... but by now he was falling asleep.

END

FIRST THE HISTORY. He had an apartment in New York, was leaving the city, and wanted someone to take over the lease. He put an ad in the *Times*, lots of people called and said they were interested because the rent was low for a one-bedroom and the location was good. He made arrangements for eight people to see the place: someone at 9, a couple at 10, a young woman and her mother at 11, and so on. To the rest of the callers he said if none of the people he was seeing tomorrow worked out he'd contact them in the order they called. He was going to sublet the place to the first person who showed he could pay the rent the next fourteen months, give two months security and whose references checked out. He wasn't going to sell the apartment—key money it's called, which he could have: the rent was that cheap. He just wanted his rent covered till the end of his lease, which would include a 10 percent surcharge to the landlord for letting him sublet.

Then a woman called; it was around 5 o'clock. She just saw the ad, doesn't know how she could have missed it before, since she got the Sunday real estate section as early as she could on Saturday and pored over it half a dozen times, but please don't tell her the apartment's been rented. He said it hasn't: today he's just taking calls, tomorrow he'll be seeing the first eight people interested in it in the order they called, so the best he can do for her now is take down her name and phone number— She cut in and asked him to describe the apartment and tell her the rent. "Really," he said, "I'll do that if I call you. But because there are so many people before you, I don't really see the possibility—" and she said "Please, the briefest of descriptions—keep it to a sixty-second minute if you want, and if I see it isn't what we're looking for, I'll be out of your hair for good." He quickly described it and said what the rent would be and she said "Excuse me, I know this is despicable to ask, though you can look on it as a sure sign of how desperate I am, but you have to let me see it today before anyone else. How can I convince you, especially when it's probably against your principles and better judgment to let a pushy aggressive person come first and, if she liked the apartment, to assume responsibility for your rent. But you also have to know I'm not typically like this. Or I am, but only for something this important. Because your place seems like the dream dwelling we've been searching for for more than a year. Everything about it including its proximity to the park and that it's in walking distance of our jobs." He said it wouldn't be fair to the previous callers, some of whom said they've also been looking a long time. Besides, the place is a mess—he's planning to give it a thorough cleaning early tomorrow—and he's going out in an hour and won't be back till late tonight. She said "Listen, if what I'm about to say doesn't work, I'll give up. I didn't want to use this sob story, but it might be the only thing to convince you. We live in a hotel, my husband and I—have since we relocated to New York—and it's depressing and dangerous, in the type of characters they get there, but the best we can afford, though it isn't cheap either. We want to move to an afford-able apartment for all the obvious reasons, but also so we can have a baby before it gets too late for me to. And your place and building and neighborhood and even the school district—I've done research on these except your apartment and building, but I know your block and love it—are ideal for that. I'd almost rent it sight unseen, but you'd think me crazy and reject me outright as a potentially unreliable sub-lessee. Please, just a peek. I don't care about the mess. I'll cab right over. What can I say that'll change your mind? We'll name our first child after you. I'm kidding, of course, but its middle name will definitely be your first or last one, or a slight rewording of it, since I don't even know your name yet and our first and possibly only child could be a girl. He said "All right, okay, what do you want me to say, but I can't promise I'll give you first crack at the place if you like it. But if I do you'll have to help me out in what to say to all the people coming tomorrow." She said "Oh, my gosh, I'm so happy. Even if I realize you haven't consigned the apartment to us, I feel that if we do get it we'd be taking over a very benevolent and hospitable home, one where there'd be an aura of generosity and kindness so pervasive that—" and he said "No more, please. If I let you go on I'm sure I'll end up not even taking rent from you. Besides, I get uncom-fortable when people speak well of me, and I'm not any of the things you say, nor is my apartment," and she said "Just know I understand how troubling the decision to let me see it now was for you, so you have the deepest thanks not only from me but my husband Dennis."

She rang the bell in twenty minutes, flew through the apartment, saying "Oh, this is beautiful... wonderful... what a great bathroom... a working fireplace too? I'm glad you didn't say so in your ad, because even more people would have called. If you stick your head out the window I bet there's a view of the park," and he said "I've tried it from every window; doesn't work and not worth the risk finding out." She said "Obviously, I love the apartment and will give you not one but three months' rent in advance plus the two months' security you're asking for if that's what it'll take to sublet it. Not that giving you so much money won't deplete our savings and checking accounts and also our parents'—we both come from lower-working-class families— and put us in debt," and he said "Don't you want your husband Daniel—" "Dennis," she said. "Daniel was my third husband. Only kidding and not much of a joke. It must be I'm trying to make them to please you." "Dennis to see it and give his okay?" and she said "He trusts my instincts in these matters and said he'd go along with any decision I made. Since I'm ecstatic at the prospect of living here, I'm positive he'll be impressed with it too and also happy I'm so thrilled with it." "Okay, then," he said, "and forget about going into debt. If your references check out, the place is yours. Though I'll have to have both your signatures on the sublease and one month's security, which, if there are no damages to the place that I have to pay for, I'll return to you at the end in full, with regular bank interest for it. But please, if you can have the rent to me by the first of every month so I can send the landlord my check without having my own bank accounts depleted, it'd be greatly appreciated. I live kind of on the margin myself." "Dennis does all our household bill-paying, check-writing, and taxes and is meticulous and punctual about those things, so you can be sure he'll be right on top of it." Their references checked out, he made up a sublease and mailed it to them, they had it notarized, something he should have thought of himself since it probably also benefited him, and returned it by registered mail. She came by for the keys and to give him the first month's rent and a month's security, and the day after he moved out, they moved in.

She wrote him once in the next three years saying they'd found a number of his things in the apartment and did he want her to send him them: a silver fountain pen, key ring with keys, folded-up ten dollar bill in the back of his desk drawer, letter-size envelope with several old photos in it of people in their twenties and thirties, and what looked like a valuable Victorian stickpin. He wrote back saying how about if he picked them up next time he was in New York and in the meantime would she keep them in a safe place?—the photos are of his parents and he didn't realize he no longer had them, the stickpin was his mother's parents' wedding gift to his father and he long ago gave up on finding it along with the fountain pen he bought in Germany at a reasonable price and was close to being a talisman to him but much too expensive to replace in the States: Where in God's name did she find them? And she wrote back a postcard saying "Will do as requested regarding your treasures. This may sound strange, though be assured there's nothing mystical or uncanny about him, but Dennis has a way of accidentally turning up people's lost articles. Once—it's too complicated to go into in so small a space—he found something in a sink pipe he was replacing in his parents' home that a good friend of his claimed to have lost in a lake two hundred miles away."

He called them soon after he moved back to the city—he'd been back on short visits a few times and much as he wanted the photos, stickpin and pen he could never find the time to contact them—and made an appointment with her to go to their apartment. Dennis wasn't there; he was taking a night school course to learn data processing. I. complimented her on the way they'd turned his dreary hovel into a cheerful and elegant place and mostly with the same furniture and drapes he left behind, and she said "That's mainly Dennis's doing, and all the art on the walls he also made. If he thought a wall needed an abstraction, zip, he did it. And between those windows, a realistic cityscape would look good?—you got it, in one day, painted, framed, and hung. He's nowhere near to being a real painter, he says; just a capable imitator with a slight individualistic flair." They had wine and cheese—he bought the wine as a belated housewarming gift, "but I should've brought two—one to drink now and the other for you two to have later—because I'm getting back my ten bucks"—and she talked about the building and his former neighbors, some of whom are true characters, she said, and one an out-and-out pest. "Once she learned Dennis was good with his hands, she began ringing our doorbell once a week for Mr. Fix-It to fix or build something for her, and he can't find it in him to charge her or say no. It's his small-town solid large-family upbringing, which instills in you that your immediate neighbors—in his case that meant the whole town—and their idiosyncrasies and demands are to be indulged no matter what sort of manipulators, sluggards, and ingrates they are." She said they were still trying to have a child before her eggs stop dropping or the local elementary school starts deteriorating—"It's now ranked as one of the city's best, with its test scores second only to one on the Upper East Side in a school district we could never afford to live in. But I don't blame Dennis for our not conceiving yet. Nobody wants to be a father more, and his sperm count and motility, is it?, are off the charts." When he got up to leave she apologized that Dennis wasn't home yet. "He does exist, you know. I didn't invent him to make it easier for me to get your apartment, if the landlord or you had a problem, let's say, with an unattached single woman with a skimpy income subletting and then renting it. In fact," looking at her watch, "I bet he rings the downstairs buzzer any minute—that's our signal that he's on his way up and I should get rid of my gloomy puss and the empty liquor bottles and quickly spruce up the joint. If you leave now you'll probably pass him on the street or by the mailboxes downstairs, though neither of you will know who the other is and he might even suspect you of something devious if he sees you in the building. I'm of course just rambling now, hoping to stall you long enough till he gets here, because I know how much he wants to meet you. Say, what if we make a date to take you out to dinner? As thanks for your being so understanding and fair about the apartment. Letting me see it before anyone else and not jacking up the rent above the landlord's surcharge or asking us to buy the furniture you left behind, just leaving it because I said we could use it. Also, for putting in a good word to the landlord when he called you—you see, you didn't know I knew that, but he said you gave us a sterling report as tenants when he asked if we should become the new leaseholders. He didn't know you'd never met Dennis or been back to the apartment since you left it." He said "As for the landlord— your check always came to me on time and you were very nice during our first encounters and I assumed a nice husband went along with it. And sure, let's get together for dinner—I'd like to see if this guy really lives and breathes. Anyplace you want, but nothing fancy, if you don't mind, since I want to go Dutch."

They met a week later at a restaurant she chose. The food was expensive, they had a couple of bottles of good wine with and some drinks before, and Dennis and she insisted on picking up the check, though first had to grapple with him for it and then argue why they wouldn't even let him pay his share. He saw them about every other week after that: they'd invite him to parties or to their apartment for dinner or call and say—one or the other would—"What are you doing tonight? Like to go out with us for dinner or to a movie?" After they lost their two-day-old daughter—he was at the hospital with them when the doctor told them he didn't think there was anything they could do to save her— and Dennis began drinking heavily and smoking a lot of pot and they battled for a while and she moved out and they eventually divorced, Dennis became his closest friend till I. got a job in Baltimore, married, had kids, bought a house, and got back to New York less and less over the years and mainly, while she was still alive, to see his mother.

Then the call today. "Dad, phone," his younger daughter yelled. "Who is it?" he said, going to the phone, and she said "How would I know? A man." He said hello and the man said "Hi, my name's Bob Siskosski. You don't know me—" and he said "You must be Dennis's brother. Something bad's happened to him," and Bob said "That's right; he died Saturday," and was cremated yesterday, Bob said—"That's what he always told me he wanted; no funeral or religion, nothing. 'Just dump the ashes anywhere you want.' Those were his actual words; twice, so he meant them. But for my own needs, to close this thing, I'm having a memorial for him a week from Sunday in Trenton. That's not where we grew up but where I live now. My folks and sister are dead, so no reason to have it back there, and I thought Trenton was relatively convenient for Denny's friends in New York. You also, though it'll be a little longer for you to get to than them." "That's no problem. Two, maybe a two-and-a-half hour drive." He took down Bob's phone number and the phone number of the funeral home. "I'll call one of you for directions if I can make it to the memorial, which I'm almost sure I can. But my wife's quite sick, Dennis might not have mentioned it, so you never know what can come up. And thanks for contacting me. It couldn't have been easy locating all his old friends." "He had an address book by his bed and your name was in it. Maybe four to five of your addresses and phone numbers, but the last one not crossed out. You probably want to know what happened." "To Dennis, you mean?" "Maybe it's already been too much for you, what I said. I realize this can be difficult, a friend, just hearing the news. Me? I've called so many people about the memorial, and before that, right after it happened, his death, that I'm used to talking about it. It also helps me, speaking to his friends, some of them going on at such lengths about him and what a great loss that I asked them to save it for the memorial so everyone could hear. But if you don't want me to..." and he said "No, please. A part of me holds back, mainly because I think it might be too tough on you. But if you don't mind talking about it, I'd like to know." "It's pretty simple, really: he got out of bed in the morning and keeled over. That's the way it looked from the position he was in and what he was wearing. Boxer shorts, which is what he slept in since he was twelve and my mother let him instead of PJs. And that the bed was unmade, a toss-and-turn mess. You have to know what that bed means, though, to understand the whole story. I knew Denny better than anyone. We weren't the kind of brothers that double-dated and went to hookers and got drunk together. I was four years younger. But we slept in the same room all our childhood, and he always made his bed first thing after getting up, and I know he still did. The cleaning lady he had every other Saturday found him. Why he thought he needed her, I don't know, since he kept his place spotless. Or maybe he keeled over during the night. Got up, was going to the john or for a glass of water, and dropped dead—maybe grabbed his chest or something—a second or two after he got off the bed. The cleaning lady knew something was wrong when she rang from downstairs, since he never before didn't buzz her in. She rang the tenant next door to him, who she knew had a spare key to his place, and let herself in and saw him and called the police. He really admired you, I want to say to you now, if I don't have the time to at the memorial. That is, if you come to it, because I know your situation. The way you kept to your work all those years with no compensation. He said a few times he would have liked giving up his regular job to become a filmmaker—said this after the baby died and his marriage busted up—but didn't have what you did to do it... you know, keep his seat stuck to the chair, or whatever they'd say for making films. Maybe the same thing if you're writing a script, which is also what he wanted to do and maybe did, though I haven't found any yet. He would have been good at it too—all of filmmaking—don't you think? Terrific eye for things and good with dialog when he told stories, and he knew how to be brief while also being entertaining. And he knew people; he was insightful without being a dried-up psychologist." "That's true, he was. Very sharp and he saw things clearly, what people did and motivated them and so on. When he read a book—he didn't read them much, he'd be the first one to tell you, and it often took him half a year for a normal-size book—even a short one sometimes, like Camus' *The Stranger*. But when he did he was original in his reading of it, telling me things I hadn't seen before in the book but which were right on target, more than almost anyone I knew, college professors and the rest of them." "That could be so; we didn't talk books, and as kids we didn't read many either and weren't encouraged to. Our folks were uneducated; I don't even think we had a Bible, and if we did it was never pulled out. But I also want to tell you that he said you were one of his two or three best friends." "Thanks. For a while, that's what we were. Maybe for me, for about ten years, he was my best. Never an argument between us. Always lots of laughs and some really good conversations about lots of things, and he was loyal too. I don't want to go into it, but there were times. And helping me paint my place, and when I had a car, fixing it, and things like that. Then I moved down here—I'm talking twenty years ago—and we saw each other much less, not that we wanted it like that. But you know, my wife, and I have kids and more and more I had to take care of them, and my teaching work and the work I try to do outside of it, and God knows what else—it's been a crazy twenty years—so what can you do?"

After the call, he told his wife, said "I don't know what it is, but I'm not sad, though I know I'll miss the guy," and she said "Probably because it hasn't sunk in yet. I'm sorry. He was a nice happy-go-lucky unpretentious man and a good friend to you, I'll say that much for him, even if he didn't like me very much," and he said "What are you talking about?" and she said "I could tell. The few times we were with him together. Even at our wedding reception when he gave us a meat cleaver as a gift—" and he said "He was an exceptional cook and it was an expensive cleaver— Hammacher Schlemmer... some good store like that—and he knew I liked to cook and assumed you did to, or I told him," and she said "Admit it. It was a strange wedding gift. And to hand it to you in a paper bag and want you to look at it right there? All right, it was our apartment we had the reception in. Anyway, he hardly… what did we do with the cleaver? Because I don't recall seeing it again." "I put it away and then threw it out. Wrapped it in cardboard so it wouldn't cut the people who took the garbage. I knew neither of us would ever use it, and the damn thing scared me. But it was a well-intentioned present, and practical for cutting certain things we didn't cook, like duck and short ribs and whole fish, dishes he thought I should try cooking but needed the right tools for. He asked me a few times about the cleaver and if I was using it and I always said I was. I could never have told him that I'd thrown it out." "Anyway," she said, "he hardly ever looked at me and would usually only respond to you, even if I was the one who asked him something. And when he called here he never gave me more than five seconds before he asked for you." "Certainly more than that. It'd take five seconds just to say hello, how are you, and am I home, because Dennis was always civil, and then your reply to him and maybe something polite in return." "Ten seconds, then. You know what I'm saying. He didn't like my looks, for one thing. I had the feeling—and this from someone who was no great shakes as a looker himself—that he thought every woman he or one of his friends went out with—and married? You bet!—had to be peerlessly beautiful. With a tiny nose, or at least not a so-called Jewish one, and huge bosom and long slim legs and perfect ass, like you said his wife was and had, though you never mentioned her behind." "Believe me—and the stuff about the nose is, well, in that respect I did have a bit of trouble with, but then he himself said he came from a conventionally biased

family in a region of the country where there were no
Semites of any kind and small noses were the norm, or that's
what they wanted him to believe. But he overcame all that
and I think long before he left his hometown. And every
time I spoke to him, he asked after you and said what a bum
deal you got. That's how he put it. Once even calling just to
tell me of some new treatment for it he'd read in a magazine,
which we already knew of for a couple of years and didn't
work on you. But that was good of him, right? It's possible
he felt so bad for you that he didn't want to ask you about
your health, or sickness, knowing beforehand what he'd
hear, if you were frank with him. And if it had been an especially rough day for you—or week, or month, which I'd spoken of to him—even worse. So he asked me about you, and
that was enough, wasn't it? First or second thing when we
talked on the phone. And when my mother was alive, same
thing: 'How is she?' And before you got sick, maybe he didn't
think you thought he had a good mind, so he felt somewhat
reserved with you, or inferior, or something. No, that could-
n't have been. He knew he was smart and sharp in his own
way and that you were no snob. As for his wife, who was
quite lively and quick-witted and pleasant, she *was* very
pretty and bosomy and leggy and so forth, but he never said
all women should be like that. Sure, it'd be nice to have if it
was part of the whole package—any guy would tell you—
but it wasn't mandatory with him. He used to say he got
lucky when he met her and unlucky when she dropped him
or just very stupid and lazy when he let her leave so easily,
for if there was any bad luck it was all in losing their child.
But illusions about himself? No more than anyone to keep

yourself going. But I felt lucky to have them as friends then. At the time I was nearly broke and didn't know anyone in the city to be close with and they knew it and I'm sure saw me as someone a bit lost and sort of took me in." "Oh, stop it. They wanted you as a friend because they liked you and you were serious and smart. I think another reason he didn't care much for me was that he blamed me for keeping you from moving back to New York. Your job here. That I, all right, nagged you after your first two years when you were thinking of giving it up, to stick with it if you wanted to marry and have kids. He felt you had enough experience by then to land a similar job in New York. I don't think he realized you were fortunate to get the job in the first place, with no advanced degree or previous teaching, and that finding a comparable one in a city with a thousand people with your credentials and perhaps more teaching experience and publications would be next to impossible," and he said "I don't know if he didn't realize that. He thought if I adopted his tactics in applying for a job, which entailed pushing myself in ways I didn't like and padding and even lying on my CV, I'd be able to get one. I also don't know if I was so unemployable the first time around," and she said "You tried, didn't you? When you hit forty, two years before we met, you said you'd had it with scrounging for low-paying jobs and felt you had enough publications and practical experience in the field to get a full-time college position. So you sent I don't know how many letters and résumés to colleges and even to a few private high schools in the New York area—" "Fifty-three, to be exact." "God, the paperwork involved. And you said you didn't use a copier for any of the letters either." "I thought my chances would be better with an original copy, the school and department's names on it, etcetera—you know, the personal touch." "Only two wrote back. One from someone—Columbia, General Studies—you'd known years before and didn't know he'd gone into teaching and now ran the writing department there, so you figured he was only being polite. And both said they'd put your résumé in their job file, which you said was another name for trash pile." "That's because, other than for saying in my letter to the City College department that that school was my alma—that was the other one that wrote back—I was doing it all wrong, as Dennis kept reminding me. I just sent out to these departments willy-nilly. I didn't first learn through professional journals if they had openings, and if I was just sending out haphazardly, who the department chairs were so I could address them by name and proper job title. I also didn't write my CV in the accepted format. Didn't even know what a CV was. There's a way to do it and a way to screw it, he said, and I was acting like a greenhorn at it, and my cover letters were too informal and long. He also said I should call soon after I sent the letter to see if it arrived and what were the chances of getting an interview. In other words to show my eagerness for the job and also to make personal contact with them. Calling up the chairman, in fact, through his direct number and then saying I'd asked College Information for the department's secretary, since I didn't want to disturb him, but as long as I got him on the phone… So he could get a feel of me and see I was articulate and respectful and not, with that department secretary line, pushy. Anyhow, I didn't follow his advice—at the time all those procedures seemed too stiff and calculating for me. But I did the second time around with the job I have now, and with that one I listened to you both when I learned of the opening and applied. But let's be honest. I never would have got it if the woman who was originally hired didn't bow out a month before the semester started and they needed someone fast. But to get back to what we were talking about before, we both agree that a hell of a nice guy died before his rightful time or something—that sounds so dumb, but you know what I mean." "He was very likable and it's a great shame and I'm truly sorry. But you're okay about it? Sort of? Talking about him helped?" and he said "I don't know why but I still don't feel anything. I should; he was a wonderful friend and we went through a lot. I should have a mass of memories pouring in and some that overwhelm me, as they did when... what the heck was his name who died—my friend from California whom you met once when he visited—and his ex-wife called to tell me?" "Jason?" "Jackson Mead. I even remember we were listening to a Corelli concerto grosso—that Deutsche Grammophon recording you had and which I played so much, and after the call I couldn't stop crying, and he wasn't half the friend Dennis was." "We were having dinner when she called, I remember, so you probably had some wine with it and a drink or two before. And the music was mournful, if it's the piece I'm thinking of, though most of the Opus 6 on that recording can be moving with or without alcohol. So when her call came, and it was as unexpected as this one... ah, why try to analyze it?" "That's what I say. But to answer your question? This little talk… though not so little—certainly not short, and I don't know if it's what I needed, and maybe not even what I meant by that. I'm obviously a bit confused now, which might be part of it: the shock of hearing that he died. I suppose it was good to talk about him and get a few things out. I think that's right, but… oh, well," and he bent over and kissed the top of her head while she patted the back of his neck.

Later, while drinking his second vodka and grapefruit juice in the living room and reading the newspaper, his younger daughter asked him to read to her. *Kristin Lavransdatter;* they'd been reading it almost every night for three months and were near the end of the second book. He went into her room with his drink, said "Ready?" and she nodded and he closed the door so they wouldn't be disturbed, flicked the wall light switch that turned off her night table light, sat across the room beside the lamp on her desk, and opened the book to the bookmark. "Maybe you can remind me where we left off," he said. "After I finish reading I always think I'll remember the next day the last part I read, but my memory's become terrible. Oh, let's just start at the top of the first complete paragraph," and he started to read but after a few sentences his throat constricted and he couldn't go on. He also had trouble seeing the print because his eye glass lenses had misted up. He took his glasses off and wiped them. "What's the matter, Daddy?" and he tried speaking but couldn't and cleared his throat and said "I'm sorry, sweetheart, but not tonight. I'm too sad to read." "I know, but what about?" and he started to cry and covered his eyes with his hand and wiped them and coughed his throat clear again and said "Do you remember… there, that's better," and closed the book on his finger, thinking maybe he'd be able to read after he finished talking to her. "Do you… no, you wouldn't. You only met him a few times over the last dozen years when we were with Grandma at Ruppert's in New York, and the last time had to be more than two years ago," and she said "Your friend Dennis? He die?" "You remember him?" and she said "Sure, he was so lively." "That's amazing. Usually when I mention people of the past—people we've spent a lot more time with than Dennis, even—you say you've no idea who I'm talking of." "No, he was funny; I liked him. Too bad he died. You hear it today?" and he nodded because he felt his throat constricting again and she said "No wonder you're sad. You don't have to read to me tonight. It's all right." "Thanks," and he went over to her bed and kissed her forehead, put the bookmark back in the book, grabbed his drink off the desk and turned off the lamp and closed the door. How'd she know, though? Overheard them talking or his wife told her? The door across the hall to his older daughter's room was slightly open, the room dark, and he stuck his head in and said "Excuse me, but you're in bed too? It's so early for you. You must be tired. Goodnight, my darling," and she said goodnight. He should go in, kiss her as he did his other daughter, but her room's always a mess and he might trip over something. "Oh, one thing… you still up?" and she said yes and he went into the room, stood by the door and said "Do you remember my friend Dennis?" "The very tall one in New York? Yes, why?" and he said "You remember him too. I'm curious as to why. You both only met him at Ruppert's when we used to take Grandma there during our Christmas breaks and in June when we were in the city." "And sometimes on the street going and coming from Grandma's and once when we were all sitting in the park and he walked by," and he said "Those times too. But not for long, is what I'm saying, in the restaurant or on the street. And the park one we only just waved, if I'm not mistaken. He looked in a hurry to get someplace and I think we'd just seen him in Ruppert's an hour before, sitting at the bar in that little corner place by the pay phone—his office, he used to say, because that's where he always sat, if one of the stools there was free, and made and got lots of calls." "Still, I remember him. He laughed a lot and loud and liked to kid around with us. He also made you laugh, and Grandma. Did something happen to him? By the way you're talking and your voice…" and he said "He died a few days ago; I only found out today." "Oh gee, I'm sorry. What happened?" and he said "His heart or a blood clot to the brain." "He was such a nice man. I remember you said he was the one person you knew who helped you out with Grandma without you asking him, other than your family." "What did I mean? How did he help?" and she said "Like when we met him on the street. Pushing the wheelchair for you or helping us get it up the curb. And in the restaurant, helping us get Grandma into a seat and putting the wheel-chair away." "That's right, he did it all the time when we bumped into him at Ruppert's. He would come over with his coffee or drink—usually a drink—and sit down with us till our food came. Probably not staying longer because he knew we'd be bothered by his smoking while we ate, though Grandma wouldn't or the restaurant didn't want him smoking there. And then when it was obvious we were getting ready to leave he'd come over again to say goodbye and help with Grandma—those darn double doors to the street, for instance; they were hard getting her through walking and next to impossible in the chair." "You could tell he was a good friend of yours even if you didn't see him as much as the way people see their good friends." "I know and that's one of the reasons I'm feeling kind of sad," and he started choking up and the tears again and wiping them and she said "You okay?" and he said "Yeah, and I hope you don't mind, but I just have to tell you this. I didn't really act to him as well as I should have since I moved down here, or at least since I got married and Mommy moved down a year after. That's the truth. I should have seen him more often. But I was so busy—I'm not trying to give this as an excuse. Getting married, having you girls, my work here, seeing Grandma a lot and even the majority of the time we were in New York—every other day whenever we were there, at least for a couple of hours—and of course Mommy getting sick. That maybe more than anything else the last ten years." "So? You couldn't help it," she said. "You had other important things to do," and his younger daughter yelled from her room "Be quiet; I'm trying to sleep." "I *was* busy," he whispered, "but not that much to neglect everything else for that long. So you could say I pretty much ignored him. He wanted to see me. He called plenty, maybe five times a year, and I don't think I called him five times from Baltimore in all my years here." "But you did when you were in New York." "Infrequently, though, and usually with an excuse why I couldn't see him, and, to be honest with you, sometimes lies. But when he called, we always had a long conversation, if I wasn't tied up in this house with something else then or my schoolwork to do, and Dennis as usual doing most of the talking. Not because he hogged the call. I just don't talk much on the phone or even much like to be on it." "So that's okay if you do that," and he said "I know; I'm not saying it isn't. But listen. After we had talked awhile, Dennis, as I said, doing most of it—and some of what he said was very interesting and smart. The guy had ideas and opinions and theories about everything, it seemed—solutions too—though most of it was about things he'd read in the paper recently—he'd say 'When you coming to New York?' Or 'When you next come to the city, give me a buzz'—a call—'a few days before so we can plan on getting together. Even if it's tax time, I'll make room.' That's what he ended up working at: preparing taxes for people. From his apartment, He did all right too. He learned how to do it by working for a tax service a short time and then started up his own business—just him—and earned enough during the three to four months of tax season to live fairly well the rest of the year. I remember the business cards and flyers he designed for it, a new one every year. They were quite clever. He always sent them to me, not so he could do my taxes but to see if I liked them, and a couple of times sketches of them and if I thought the wording and grammar were right or the jokes referring to taxes or tax preparers weren't too gross. I remember one with a chicken but I forget what it was about. As to his living entirely off this work, I think he also finagled getting

unemployment insurance twenty weeks a year by paying
one of his businessman-clients to say he was employed by
this man. Or not paying but exchanging his tax services for
it. Some deal—in fact I know it's so because he told me—
where Dennis also gave this man the equivalent of what
would be his Social Security and Medicare deductions and
whatever other payroll taxes and deductions would be taken
out of his made-up paychecks for half a year's work he never
did for this man... anyway, it's complicated. But he swung
it, something I didn't particularly go for—let's face it, it
was dishonest—but okay, that's what he did and he never
got caught. As to why I didn't see him when he wanted to
meet, I don't know what the reason was. Was it because
I didn't find him as interesting and amusing and compan-
ionable as I once did? Or if his drinking, which got heavier
and heavier over the years, and for sure during the off-tax
season, became tiring and irritating to deal with, or what?
Though when I did bump into him at Ruppert's or someplace I was always glad to see him and we had a good time,
quick as it was. Maybe because you kids were usually with
me, and Grandma, so there were distractions and I could
play off you all and it wasn't just Dennis and me. Now the
guy's dead and I feel like a real heel—a rat, a louse, a bastard, quite honestly. I'm sorry, I hate using that word in
front of you, but that's what I really was, a lousy bastard
that I didn't see him more. Made some effort to, because
I know that once we started talking—and it didn't have to
be over a drink, which is what we used to do; it could have
been coffee; like every big drinker, he also loved coffee—it
would have been all right and even ended up being a good

time. And it would have made him feel good too, because—"
and his younger daughter yelled from her room "Please,
I'm still trying to get to sleep and I still can't. You're talking too much and loud again," and he shut the door—
"Should have done that before"—and whispered "Because,
what? Because I know he knew I was ignoring him, yet he
still called me because he thought—he must have—that
once we got together we'd have a long easy talk with lots of
laughs and so on like in the old days. There were plenty of
things we could have talked about after all that time of not
really seeing each other. But I did wrong. I know I did.
I made him feel like crap by not once in around ten years
calling him up when I was in town, and he knew we stayed
in New York every Christmastime and for a few weeks in
June and came in lots of other weekends, and saying 'Let's
not just rely on occasionally bumping into each other at
Ruppert's. Let's meet, there or anyplace you want, and have
lunch and talk.' Oh, well…" and he looked at her in the
dark and said "You up, sweetheart? Did I put you to sleep?"
and she didn't answer and he wiped his eyes, because he'd
been crying while he was talking but hadn't noticed it till
now, and left the room and shut the door and when he got
to the living room, quietly blew his nose.